UNDER THE
EVENING
SKY

FINN
CARLING

UNDER THE
EVENING
SKY

Translated
from the Norwegian and
with a Foreword by Louis A. Muinzer

PETER OWEN
London and Chester Springs PA

PETER OWEN PUBLISHERS
73 Kenway Road London SW5 0RE

Peter Owen books are distributed in the USA by
Dufour Editions Inc. Chester Springs PA 19425–0449

Originally published as *Under aftenhimmelen*
First published in Great Britain 1990
© Finn Carling 1985
English language translation copyright © Louis A. Muinzer 1990

ISBN 0–7206–0783–3

Typeset by Selectmove of London
Printed in Great Britain by Billings of Worcester

TO MY SON
PREBEN

Foreword

ALTHOUGH he is an offbeat and highly original Norwegian writer, Finn Carling can only be summed up by one of literature's most hackneyed clichés: he is, simply, a Man of Letters. There seems no other way to characterize an author of prose and verse, fiction and plays, travel books and memoirs, along with works on a variety of social and psychological subjects. For all its diversity, however, Carling's writing has a coherence and a depth that give it a special place in his country's literature. Both unexpected and inimitable, it gained for its author Norway's major literary award, the Aschehoug Prize, in 1987.

Yet although Finn Carling's career has been an impressive one, its achievements have not been easily gained. The writer, born in the Oslo suburb of Smested in 1925, is a victim of cerebral palsy, and his life has been the battle of a brave spirit against the inadequacies of his body. Nevertheless, far too much can be made of his handicap, which should not be viewed as a physical condition but rather as a catalyst – a source of insight and creative power to be drawn upon in a variety of sometimes unsuspected ways.

Carling made his literary début in 1949 with *Broen* (The Bridge), a volume of stories and a short play. In a series of early works he established himself firmly as a writer before probing his personal disability directly in *Kilden og muren* (And Yet We Are Human). Written in English in the late 1950s and published in Great Britain in 1962, this forthright and never self-pitying book was an acknowledged breakthrough that freed the maturing writer to explore new areas and levels of experience. Thereafter, in such books as *Blind verden* (Blind World, 1962) and *De homofile* (The Homosexuals, 1965), he was able to write with deep insight about the nature of others who seem walled off from the 'average' and the 'ordinary'. Even more important, however, he came to understand that the condition of such outsiders is in essence the condition of our race: that to be human is to be handicapped, whether in body, personality, social situation or common mortality. In short, Carling's striking personal background is no more, and no less, important than the body of experience every important writer must use as the bridge between himself and the world in which and for which he writes. In his ripest work Finn Carling simply explores us all; with implicit sympathy, but with an awareness of our flawed existence, he evokes our dreams and our vulnerabilities with the heart of a sharer and the eye of an artist.

But no amount of generalization can do justice to a distinctive literary talent: Finn Carling must be read, not talked about. The present translation offers English readers their first opportunity to sample Carling's fiction and to discover for themselves why he is considered one of Norway's most inventive and original writers. Choosing a single work for that purpose is not easy, for Carling is a productive writer and the candidates for translation are fairly numerous. Yet for a first Carling read, few of his works could equal *Under the Evening Sky*, a characteristically short novel first published as *Under aftenhimmelen* in Norway in 1985. Less complex in structure than *Fiendene* (The Enemies, 1974), for instance, and (seemingly) more realistic than *Fabel X* (1984), this curious book is as accessible and as entertaining as a good detective story, with a deft and unexpected climax. Apparently casual and episodic, the novel brings together two monumentally ill-matched strangers who dine together for five evenings on a Greek island and swap stories. As the evenings pass, Carling unobtrusively welds the tales into a single tale about the tellers, displaying both his own talent as a story-teller and his skill as a literary craftsman. Here, too, we encounter his flair for characterization and the building of dramatic incident, as well as his distinctive blending of dark humour, social satire, fantasy and fellow-feeling, which never slackens into sentiment.

In *Under the Evening Sky* Norwegian readers familiar with Finn Carling's work will also find a wide deployment of the author's favourite themes, such as imagination and reality, art as a personal process and social fetish, and man's need to escape from the prison of his loneliness. Among the more specific motifs featured in the individual episodes, they will notice Carling's concern with modern family life and his fascination with animals as a key to our humanity, a subject pursued with tragic power in his play *Gitrene* (The Bars, 1966) and with domestic intimacy in *Merkelige Maja* (Strange Maja, 1989), a recent book about his own pet dog. The new reader, though, will not be much concerned with recurring themes and motifs, but will want a story that makes him read it because it takes place somewhere within his own experience and involves him in ways he cannot quite identify. *Under the Evening Sky*, with its resonant tales and its strangely knowable characters, is just such a book.

In preparing the first English text of a Carling novel I have been greatly assisted by two men. One is Michael Levien, whose expert editorial guidance and stylistic revisions have improved my translation in many matters of detail. The other is Finn Carling himself, a patient friend of more than two decades, who responded to numerous queries about his Norwegian text and my re-creation of it in a new language. In accordance with his wishes, and in conformity to the text of the original, this narrative of curious table talk is printed without quotation marks. Finally, I wish to thank Juliet Standing for her assistance in the rendering of the Greek dishes that are served up so generously in the novel, as Carling's characters and readers dine together under the evening sky.

Louis A. Muinzer

CONTENTS

THE FIRST
EVENING

ROBERT TURNER'S meeting with the emaciated man, who after a moment's hesitation had introduced himself as Joseph Frost, one lovely May evening at a little restaurant on an island in the Aegean Sea, was quite accidental. Though one never knows. It could be that Robert Turner had given the waiter the impression he would like company at dinner and that the emaciated man had therefore been guided imperceptibly to the table where Robert Turner was absently studying the menu. It could also be that the man calling himself Joseph Frost had been unconsciously drawn to the stranger. That the erect form with the short-clipped grey beard and a half-raised wineglass had given him a vague presentiment that something unusual might happen and that the waiter had instantly perceived this in his glance.

No one will ever know for sure.

Yet Robert Turner showed no sign of surprise when the emaciated man hesitantly introduced himself as Joseph Frost and asked if the seat at his table was free. An outsider observing them from a distance would simply have thought that they were two friends who were going to dine together and that one of them had accidentally been late. That it is always unpleasant to sit waiting could have explained their reserved behaviour and the fact that the emaciated man didn't sit down but merely remained standing while he seemed to be awkwardly explaining something. Was he trying to excuse himself for arriving so late?

Of course he wasn't doing so, for neither of them had seen the other before. After a time, Robert Turner extended his hand and greeted the emaciated man, and the outside observer would perhaps have imagined, with relief, that his lateness had been excused. That everything was now as it had been before. But that was precisely what it wasn't: the outsider wouldn't have heard what the men had been saying.

You tell me, observed Robert Turner drily, without my immediately being able to understand why, quite unprompted, you volunteer such confidences to a complete stranger, that you are suffering from some kind of terminal illness. Moreover, that you have left your family for good without saying a word about where you were going. If that was to make an impression on me, so that I would offer you my table companionship out of fellow-feeling, I can only assure you that you haven't succeeded. I've been dead once myself, so death doesn't move me. It's a highly overrated business. Rather vulgar, to boot. And yet, because I value human destinies that are a trifle out of the ordinary, I suggest that you be – shall we say – my dinner guest during the short time I intend to remain on this island. I have already ordered a *kakavia*, a special bouillabaisse that the fishermen out here cook in clay pots. You will undoubtedly find it tasty.

But that wasn't what I had in mind at all. You mustn't think. . . .

Robert Turner smiled faintly. I shan't conceal the fact that I consider it a privilege to eat with me, he said. That perhaps sounds a trifle self-confident, but I've gradually acquired an uncommonly good knowledge of the food on these beautiful islands, so, if you follow my advice, you will be able to share in some quite exquisite meals. But one gets nothing for nothing. In return for the gastronomic peaks you will experience in my company, I insist on utter frankness from you in our dinner conversation. For the very reason that we don't know each other and shall never become friends, that should be quite possible. As you will no doubt have learned in life, it is only from people who are near to one that one has anything to conceal. If you can't agree to my modest proposal, I must unfortunately ask you to leave.

The emaciated man was disconcerted. Not by the stranger's behaviour, but by his own feelings, and he reddened at the thought of the proposal, for, after all, he had introduced himself as Joseph Frost and said he was mortally ill and had left his family for good. So he remained standing with his hand on the chair-back as if he had no right to sit down. And he heard himself stammering. Which he couldn't remember doing since he was a child.

Utter frankness. I don't know what you mean. Naturally, if I don't like the food you suggest, I'll tell you so politely. Why shouldn't I?

Robert Turner laughed. The food! Good lord, that's not what I'm thinking of. What you happen to like or dislike of the food I recommend doesn't interest me. It's you as a human being who attracts my attention. There's nothing more interesting than people. What they feel, what they think, and why they act as they do. Taken all in all, that's the only thing that's made life worth living.

Hesitatingly, like a young boy who still feels uncertain that his lies and petty stealing won't be discovered, the emaciated man sat down at the table. I'm not very interesting, he mumbled.

Well, said Robert Turner, you've already told me you've left your former life because of your terminal illness. Not many have done that, you know. Most people cling to their families when they learn they're at death's door. That's something which distinguishes men from animals. A dying animal seeks dignified solitude, while a man in a comparable situation shamelessly exploits those nearest him to the limits, to gain some sense of life and belonging.

Besides, he continued, there's no such thing as an uninteresting person. I remember, for instance, a woman who also sat at my table, once. That was on Paros, by the way, and we ate an excellent mousaka, with aubergine grown in some old monastery gardens. It was as if the monks' piety had materialized from the splendid smell of the aubergines. She was, perhaps, not quite young, but dazzlingly beautiful in a cool, transparent way – as if she had been created by Botticelli in an especially felicitous moment. Indeed, I feel certain that if she had visited an art gallery – something I later learned she had never done – even the most beautifully painted women who had enchanted visitors for centuries would have blushed for shame over their own imperfection. . . . Well, this woman said precisely the same as you, that there was nothing interesting about her, and she added – as if to support her contention – that she had never done a day's work, that she lived quite alone and wasn't bound to anyone. She was an empty space, she said.

Robert Turner stopped and observed his table companion as a magician may hesitate a moment to give his audience a chance to discover how he is doing his trick. Then he continued: What touching naïvety! What unique blindness not to see the interest that lay precisely in the conflict between her rare beauty and the empty space she thought she was! There had to be an explanation for it, and while I ate the mousaka I considered how I should uncover her secret. If I had been a psychologist or psychiatrist – which thank God I'm not – I would possibly have asked aggressive questions. Would have confronted her with herself, as they say. But so crude a method is against my nature. It would have been like eating an exquisitely prepared pheasant with one's bare fingers. Instead, I displayed a *lack* of interest – gave the impression that I thought it reasonable that she had never worked, that she lived alone and that she wasn't tied to anyone. Quite cautiously, as carefully as one uncovers an old, overpainted work of art, I allowed her to feel that I was actually quite indifferent to her life.

As if to conceal a little smile, or perhaps to give his listener a chance to express his admiration for the other's rare knowledge of humanity, Robert Turner raised his glass and slowly sipped his wine. But his guest said nothing. After a while Robert Turner put his glass down.

As you have undoubtedly grasped, he continued, my demonstrative indifference had its desired effect. It is precisely the so-called self-effacing sort of person who is offended by a confirmatory lack of interest. There is a kind of personality that has to give the impression that it's absolutely nothing! To say she blushed would be to insult her, for her self-control was admirable. But her cheeks took on a darker glow, as if the skin for a moment had stolen colour from the ruby that adorned the pendant on her neck, and her eyes became a hint narrower. Then she leaned back and looked at me. Her feeling of offence had in no way subsided, but her smile disclosed that she no longer felt herself threatened and humiliated. Like a member of the cat family immediately before the spring that will crush its prey, she showed exactly how she would strike, and her weapon was truth.

After I've risen from this table, she said, we'll never see each other again, and you have no idea who I am. So I'll tell you something I've never told anyone. It's a story that you with your somewhat special kind of appetite for destinies will possibly find interesting, and in any case it may succeed in entertaining us both until the coffee comes.

Her story, said Robert Turner, who had also leaned back, was undoubtedly very interesting, but for simplicity's sake I shall venture to retell it in my own words. When she was sixteen years old, she had spent a late-summer holiday at a hunting lodge somewhere in France. She didn't say precisely where, but a few details about the landscape – which escaped her unawares – made me think involuntarily of Brittany. As a change from the strict convent school, where her family had for generations let their young girls be educated, the stay at the hunting lodge was not very rewarding. Her parents and a number of their friends, who were there too, led to be sure a life that was proper – or, if you will, improper – in those circles, but the young daughter was regarded as a child and kept outside it all with a firm hand. Her elders' amorous witticisms, their seductive embraces by the goldfish pond in the grounds and their mysterious wandering back and forth through lofty bedroom doors during the night she only experienced in glimpses from dark galleries and stairway landings and through doors left ajar. But she wasn't entirely alone, for her brother, who was one year younger, was also staying in the lodge. During the day, however, he was usually out hunting with the gamekeeper or target-shooting behind the stable or spending time with the horses and looking after them. Therefore she saw him only at meals and in the evening in what was called the children's wing. But he usually fell asleep there immediately, tired out as he was after tending the horses and his walks in the woods.

The glimpses from the galleries and stairway landings and through the cracks in doors had an unusual effect on the sixteen-year-old girl. She didn't become, as one would perhaps have imagined, filled with agonizing, sensual curiosity, and she felt no youthful disgust at the immorality she witnessed and which stood in such sharp contrast to her upbringing at the convent school. She felt only an infinite, paralysing distance between her and what she heard and saw, as if the grown-ups were beings on distant planets. The more she witnessed from her hiding-places, the more alien she felt. Not only that. Because she felt no link, no kinship, between herself and those amorously witty, embracing, nocturnal prowlers, she began to feel that she didn't exist at all. Therefore, little by little, she almost stopped eating, and the feeling she didn't exist didn't lessen when no one seemed to notice how pale and thin she had become.

So one night she seduced her fifteen-year-old brother.

When she mentioned it to me, said Robert Turner, again after a significant pause, she made a little movement with her hand, as if to indicate that it was actually a trifle, and her face was as expressionless as porcelain. But her words – and perhaps even more, her voice – said something else. Again, it wasn't a matter of sensual curiosity or in any way of sexual exploration, such as many of her friends at the convent school undoubtedly dreamt of performing and probably carried out on each other. No, what drove her on was a blind, almost unconscious, need to find a way to the world that surrounded her, and what happened – well, it was something that even what we rather rashly call mature people seldom or never experience. When she was going to describe it, she even began to falter – as if she still couldn't fully understand what had happened. That sudden encounter with another person – with her brother who was no longer a brother – thoroughly shook her. The nerves in her skin grew and enveloped that other body, made it into something much nearer than even a brother can be, and at the same time she could feel each vein, each bone, each organ in her own body. As if she saw herself from inside and could take out every single part of her body, hold it in her hand and say: That's me! And she felt a strength, as if she could at any time have lifted that little hunting lodge complete with those small, amorous people and cast it over the cliffs towards the sea.

It was, as I've said, an experience that shook her. But it didn't make the distance from the grown-ups and the world around her seem any less. The distance just became somehow switched around and even greater as well. The witticisms, the embraces, the nocturnal wanderings, which earlier had been mysterious glimpses of an enigmatic existence, were changed to helpless gestures – attempts at life that she saw through in all their vulgarity. Even her brother, whom her nerves had enveloped as a woman's long hair envelops the child at her breast, became a stranger to her afterwards, and she grew more lonely than ever. But she didn't betray it to him with a single word as he lay at her side, coolly proud of his entry into the ranks of the gamekeepers, hunters and horsemen. Ready to conquer again and again.

Then she said to Robert Turner: When dawn came, I killed him.

It sounded so ordinary and so simple – like wringing a chicken's neck – and when she told me this, she made that little movement with her hand again. All the same, I must admit that I had difficulty imagining how a sixteen-year-old girl had managed to kill her fifteen-year-old brother. So I asked her, restraining myself from making the same small, belittling hand movement, how she had set about it and why she was sitting there at my table and not in a prison cell. Then she smiled – but I'm not entirely certain if I liked that smile – and told me how, while her brother was still asleep, she had gone down and fetched a revolver from the guncase in the library. A charming little Colt with a mother-of-pearl inlaid handle, she explained, that her grandfather had brought back from America.

At cock-crow she awakened the boy, showed him the revolver and suggested laughingly that they should play at dying because of their incest. She understood her brother and knew that he was bewitched by weapons. That he had long been begging for a chance to try out that same pretty Colt. She knew too that her suggestion would appeal to his dawning conception of honour and manhood, and she said that he should first pretend to shoot her and then himself. What she didn't say, but concealed in conspiratorial, childish merriment, was that she had placed a cartridge in the chamber where it would be fired the second time he pulled the trigger. Moreover she was naked, not only because she felt this gave her power over a boy who had never seen a nude female body before but because the blood wouldn't spatter her white nightgown. When he placed the revolver beneath her left breast against her heart and pulled the trigger, she let herself fall at the foot of his bed, and with closed eyes she lay waiting for the crack of the shot against the boy's temple, where she had told him a man would shoot himself.

It came after only an instant. Then she sprang up, put on her white nightgown and positioned herself as if paralysed in the doorway of her brother's room. She was standing there when her parents and their friends – awakened by the shot – came running through the long corridors of the lodge.

Robert Turner leaned slowly forward, placed his elbows on the edge of the table and supported his chin in his hands while he said, as if to himself: She was right about our never seeing each other again, after she rose from the table at the end of dinner. Nor did I ever find out who she was.

Did you believe her?

Robert Turner looked at him sharply. Naturally. She had entered into the same agreement as yourself – one of utter frankness – so I don't know why you ask. Besides, you know, it was precisely what I saw in that lovely face of hers. Perhaps not precisely the incest and the cunning murder, but that she had a story to tell about life and death, about being close and far away.

As if Robert Turner had given the waiter a secret signal agreed upon beforehand, the bouillabaisse was then placed in front of them on the table. For a long while the two men ate in absolute silence. The distinctive fish soup, which, as it were, brought up from the depths the Aegean's most precious secrets, seemed to make everything else appear meaningless, and the emaciated guest had to admit to himself that he had seldom eaten anything that tasted so good. After the first spoonful, to be sure, he had stretched his hand out for the salt, but Robert Turner's look had restrained him: one didn't season a soup like this according to one's own whims! Slowly he also became aware that the different ingredients formed an absolutely divine harmony, and he realized what a sacrilege he had nearly committed.

When Robert Turner had finished his first helping of that excellent soup and leaned back to consider whether he would let himself be tempted to have another, his table companion bent forward a trifle uneasily and asked: Why exactly are you travelling in these islands?

Robert Turner didn't reply. Didn't move. It seemed as if his guest's words had to sink through him like shells that shine gleaming towards the bottom when one casts them into the sea. At last, he stroked his beard with a slow movement of his hand and looked up expressionlessly. That's not something told in one evening, he said.

Hesitantly, uncertainly, the guest asked: You also mentioned something about having been dead?

The one is a consequence of the other, Robert Turner said lightly. Let me put it that I, like an Orpheus, am seeking my Eurydice. Only that the situation is reversed in the sense that I rise *up* from the Kingdom of Death, not pass down to it, and that the woman I'm searching for was really a child when she came to mean something to me.

A child?

Robert Turner's eyes became quite narrow. His shoulders lifted, and his neck muscles almost burst his shirt collar. It was only for a moment, then his body relaxed and it was as if nothing had happened. He stretched his hand out for the winebottle, poured some wine for them both and put the bottle down on the table again. After that, he raised his glass and nodded to his guest so that they would drink together.

When they had both drunk, slowly and with closed eyes, Robert Turner said gently: That agreement about utter frankness naturally applies to me too, so I'll tell you how this Eurydice of mine came into my life. But first I want to warn you against drawing hasty conclusions, as you were about to do just now. . . . No, don't try to explain it away! Don't think I didn't see what you were thinking a moment ago when you asked about the child with apparent innocence. He's a middle-aged man who desires little girls, you were thinking, and you thought you could picture how I felt the little, naked body with my hands.

Suddenly he extended his hands over the table: faintly red hands with wrinkled skin and thick, slightly too long nails. The emaciated guest drew back and tried to say something but couldn't get a word out. With averted face, he glimpsed the other man bend forward and his hands extend still closer. Then he heard him ask: True, isn't it?

It came like a whiplash, and the guest pressed his shoulders against the top of the high chair-back. He tried to look at the outstretched hands, calmly, without feelings of guilt and shame, but couldn't do so. Finally Robert Turner drew back his hands, and when he spoke his voice was as gentle as before.

You needn't answer, and you must forgive me if possibly I frightened you for a moment, but I want you to understand what actually happened. I can't remember putting a hand on her, and she touched me only twice. In the churchyard where she came into my life and in the morgue when she left me.

The listener stared. In the morgue? In the churchyard?

Robert Turner smiled. You may possibly think it peculiar, but when the thought of death began to arise in my mind, I had my own burial-place prepared. I gave it a great deal of thought, and I think I may venture to say that it became unusually attractive. Flowers that once grew in the garden of my childhood encircled the grave, and where the headstone should have stood, I had a statue of a nude young girl erected – a statue it gave me great joy to reflect I was going to rest under. I found the model myself, a young dancer who would have been worthy of a Degas, and every day while the sculptor modelled her I sat in his studio and saw to it that he immortalized the charming creature.

Later I made it a custom, Robert Turner continued, to visit the grave on my little Sunday walks. After I had tended the flowers and perhaps picked a bouquet to put on my desk and remind me of the peace I had in prospect, I usually sat on a bench by the grave and let my thoughts shuttle between memories from the past and future expectations, just as many do at a graveside. I've often noticed that visitors at a churchyard tend to talk to their dear ones, as they're called, but probably seldom were. It was of course a trifle difficult in my case, in that I wasn't lying there yet. Though sometimes I would feel myself to be two people, one under the ground and one on top of it, and then a kind of conversation was possible – about my indifference to life and my acceptance of futility. About my mild contempt for those who drudge away to find a meaning, and who seek untiringly to make existence better for their fellow-men. Who haven't understood that life can only be observed, not influenced. . . . For which criteria should one then choose? By which star should one navigate?

Robert Turner looked at his guest with an eye that made it clear that this was one of those questions which simply don't admit of an answer and pointed to the steaming clay pot on the table with a movement of his hand. It is the same as with our excellent bouillabaisse, he said. We must thank our creator for its mysterious effect on our taste-buds, not try to attribute to it any philosophical meaning. And above all, he added with a little smile, we mustn't season it according to our own preconceptions.

Enough of that. One morning while I was sitting there on the bench chatting as if to my dead self, I noticed a child who was tending a grave nearby. Young people dress completely alike these days, you know, so it was a while before I realized from the child's careful movements that it must be a girl –

probably of about twelve. She had no feminine charm – at least she wasn't going to acquire any. Her features were too coarse, as in a statue by Maillol. But precisely because she was still a child, her face had the same kind of translucent, uncompromising purity that Shakespeare must have imagined when he created his Juliet, but which age inexorably muddies, just as even the clearest spring water becomes grey-brown with mud and varied putrefactions when it draws near the sea.

The girl had clearly become aware of me too, for when she looked up for a moment, she smiled. Was it because she thought she felt a bond between us? Did she see us as two lonely people in a churchyard, with sorrow as a common emotion? Regardless of what she thought, she quickly bent down again and continued tending the flowers. But plants need water, so at last she took a can and walked past my grave to a tap that wasn't far away. On her way back she stopped behind my bench and stood there with the can in her hand. We didn't look at each other, and actually I was aware of her presence only because I heard she hadn't moved on.

After a while she asked in a low voice: Is it your mother lying there?

Good lord, what should I answer? She probably thought it must be my mother because I suppose hers was lying under the meaningless flowers she was struggling to make grow on the grave a little way away. Something I never cleared up, as a matter of fact. What would have been the good? Obviously I could have answered her question in the affirmative and been done with it, but the mere thought that my mother could be lying under the beautiful nude young girl filled me with disgust. I could hardly remember where she was buried, and I had never seen her grave after I, as a young boy, had been compelled to throw a bouquet down on her coffin. A bouquet that had just been thrust quickly into my hand by my father, obviously so that a son's moving leave-taking of his mother would distract the attention of those at the burial from his own useless attempt to convey an impression of sorrow and despair. To tell the truth, it was even difficult for me to remember what she looked like when she was alive. I had only a distant memory of someone who occasionally turned up at the nursery quite unexpectedly to give the blushing nanny a reprimand, and who during the lavish garden parties that she loved to hold – entertainments that turned my fairy-tale woods into a fun-fair of noise and ballyhoo – would stretch out her arms to me invitingly, while over my head her eye searched among the guests to win their appreciation of a mother's devoted care for her son.

So I couldn't bring myself to say that it was my mother who was buried there, despite the fact that, as I've already mentioned, it would have been the simplest thing to do. On the other hand, I couldn't very well reveal to this obviously innocent child that the grave was empty, that I had intended it for myself because I was convinced that after my death no one would bother to give me such a beautiful grave, let alone look after it or sit on a bench and talk to me on Sunday mornings. And later on it was certainly confirmed that I was right. Once after my death I visited the churchyard out of sheer curiosity – it was so early in the morning there was no chance I would be discovered – and I found the grave completely overgrown and that beautiful statue smeared with bird droppings.

So I said, on a sudden whim: No, it's my daughter.

What happened then, continued Robert Turner, it's difficult for me to find words to describe to you. Not the external event but the almost shock-like effect it had on me. Suddenly I felt the child's hand stroke my cheek and remain lying on my neck. I don't know if you have ever thought about it, but children can have an appalling openness when they give of themselves which grown-ups seldom or never manage. The adult's fear of giving too much of himself – as if he were surrendering the last jewels in a secret jewel box – and gnawing suspicion that his feelings won't be returned, will almost always inhibit him. Will restrain him. . . . But the girl's hand was completely unrestrained.

How long it lay on my neck I have no idea, but it must have been a short time. Yet it felt like an eternity . . . the way a dream can make things. Glimpses from my whole life – even from my earliest, long-forgotten childhood – rose up headlong. Not in the memory, not as things remembered, but as experiences that were physically present there and then. A woman who held me in a sun-filled room, held me . . . that eternally leaping, searching child . . . held me silent against her breast. I don't remember what she looked like or who she was at all, but the warmth of the sun and the soft breast with its heartbeat inside overwhelmed me as I sat there on the bench. Once in my younger days the light touch of a trembling mouth beneath a tree in the garden did the same thing. And the longings. . . . Good lord, the longings! Arms that never embraced me, lips that never touched mine, sleepless nights spent light-years away from the person lying at my side in the darkness, and who had been lying there night after night. Pain after pain whipped through my body without stopping, without mercy.

When I came to again, like an epileptic after an attack – there's no other way to describe it – my face was wet with tears and every muscle in my body was exhausted, as if they had been stretched to breaking-point. How much the girl noticed of all this, I don't know, but there must have been something, even if she'd been standing behind me and couldn't see the tears that still streamed down my cheeks. For she said, as if to divert my attention: How beautifully you've arranged for her rest.

Fortunately, I understood what she meant. She thought I was crushed by sorrow. And perhaps I was too, I suppose, but not in the way she imagined. Not because of a rotting corpse in a grave. Sitting there, I was wishing sincerely that she would take her damned watering-can and disappear from my life. But at the same time I knew in some inexplicable way that she had become indispensable to me.

Joseph Frost – as he had introduced himself – had been sitting quite motionless, listening to Robert Turner speak. Even after this part of the story had obviously ended, he didn't dare move. It wasn't until Robert Turner finally lifted his glass and emptied it that he bent slightly forward over the table and asked: It's her you're looking for?

Robert Turner put his glass down. Yes, he replied. Of course she's no longer a child – not what she was when she disappeared from me in the morgue. But though I know it might be a great disappointment, I want to see her again. Just once. She has her story too, you know, and it might be interesting to find out how things have gone with her.

Interesting?

Robert Turner shrugged his shoulders. I can't find a better word.

But why do you think she's here, on these islands?

Because she confided in me many times, said Robert Turner, placing his napkin on the table as if to indicate that the meal was over, that she wanted to visit the Aegean islands more than anything else in the world. She wasn't a well-informed child, so naturally she had no notion of their cultural significance, but something she had probably heard or read – perhaps just seen in a picture – had created this longing in her. It would surprise me if she hasn't yielded to her longing, now that she is old enough to fulfil it.

On the way to the hotel where he was staying, the emaciated man walked along the harbour of the little town. The ruins of an old Crusaders' castle were silhouetted against the starry sky, and the lanterns on the fishing-boats and pleasure-craft made sparkling reflections in the sea. Even now, long after nightfall, there was life on the quay. On the decks of expensive seagoing sailing-ships, middle-aged men with white sweaters draped casually over their shoulders sat drinking Campari, while they idly regarded their daughters, young wives or mistresses. At the fishing-boats men arranged boxes of fish, squid and shellfish, while black-clothed women hurriedly secured slices of shark, a couple of blue mackerel or a flounder for a few drachmas before it was too late.

He walked fast, for, thanks to Robert Turner's stories, the dinner had lasted longer than when he ate alone, and he feared he wouldn't get the peace he felt he needed when he was going to write his daily letter home to his family. All the while he thought, in plain high spirits, that now he really had something to tell, that he needn't think up something new about the weather and about his wanderings through old parts of the town, but could write about that incredibly tasty soup and the man who said he had been dead and had had his own grave prepared.

As soon as he entered his room, he got out paper and pen and sat down at a small table on the balcony, where he usually sat when he wrote home. He began by telling how, as if on a sudden impulse, he had said that his name was Joseph Frost, that he was suffering from a terminal illness and had gone away without anyone knowing where. But just as he was going to write about his leaving his family, his pen stopped as if by itself and he simply sat there looking in front of him. On the way home he had laughed aloud at the thought of what they would say to each other when they read about his playful whim, about his giving the impression he was someone other than himself. About, to be precise, his playing the role of the lonely, dying man. At the sight of the words on the paper, however, he became uneasy, and it felt as if they had been written by someone else. Or by a part of himself that he hadn't known before. That frightened him, as he sat there alone under the starlit evening sky.

Tomorrow without fail, he thought, he would go and see Robert Turner and confess that the name Joseph Frost was just something he had hit upon for some unaccountable reason or other, that he was not terminally ill and that he certainly hadn't left his family for good. Afterwards he wrote a few banal lines about the ruins of the Crusaders' castle, about *la dolce vita* in the pleasure-craft as a contrast to the fishermen's eternal drudgery from early morning to late evening, and about the strangely twisted tree of Hippocrates, which grew in a little square.

Then he went out and posted the letter.

THE SECOND
EVENING

THE emaciated man, who at their first meeting had introduced himself as Joseph Frost, spotted Robert Turner the
moment he came down to the harbour. His host was sitting,
as he had done the evening before, at a table under one of the
trees outside the restaurant and letting his mildly preoccupied
eye follow the people who were walking past. This time the
guest didn't remain standing but sat down straight away, and
an outsider would have thought only that they were old friends.
Nevertheless, there was something nervous about the guest. His
thin body seemed tense, and he appeared to have difficulties
in letting his hands rest calmly in his lap or on the table. It
also appeared that he was trying to say something without
succeeding, as if his tongue wouldn't obey him, or as if it were
impossible to find the right words, but at last he was able to get
out: There's something I must tell you, but I don't know . . .

Robert Turner raised his hand. Not before I've decided
what we shall eat, he said. One musn't be side-tracked from an
important decision like that. Only when that has been made,
can we relax and our conversation begin. Yesterday we had a
splendid bouillabaisse, and today I thought we should order
arni kapamas, a dish that comes originally from Kalamata in
the southern Peloponnese and consists of lean lamb – well
sautéed, with white wine added – and sliced tomatoes, and
served with spaghetti, which *I* prefer thin. To stimulate our
appetites, I recommend that we begin with an *orektika micros*,

prawns lightly sautéed in oil and sprinkled with lemon juice, a proposal I hope you won't object to.

Besides, he added, without waiting for his guest's possible objections, I must admit that I value sharing my meals with you. Yes, I must even admit that you move me. It takes courage to go to meet death the way you've chosen – alone, as if you were really beginning a new life with no one to lean on. What is more, though perhaps it seems strange to you, I was charmed by your name. Joseph Frost! It sounds like a high-tension mixture of the South's gentle warmth and the North's biting cold. Like the name of an artist, of a man who has precisely the inner strength to shape the evening of his own life. . . . No, don't say a word! Let me guess. You're a writer, aren't you?

The guest reddened.

But my dear chap, exclaimed Robert Turner, you mustn't be ashamed of being one of the elect. Even I never managed to become one. I was merely a servant of art, an exploiting parasite some of your colleagues would probably call it, who lived in order to pass along the artistic values to students and other people who seldom or never understand. Ah, lord, what worlds they've lost!

Are you a professor?

Don't call me that, said Robert Turner. What existed before death doesn't matter any more. Titles, positions! All that is of no consequence at all afterwards. Something, of course, you will soon find out for yourself.

Then he turned to the waiter, who had stood waiting beside him for a short time, and gave his order. While hearing as if from a distance how Robert Turner assured himself of the prawns' quality and then stressed that he would accept nothing but very lean lamb, preferably from the animal's leg, the guest tried to figure out how he would admit that he had never written a line other than letters home and, on rare occasions, an account of transport problems in his work for the firm. Why in the world had he hit upon that idiotic name? Frost. He knew he'd heard it somewhere, or seen it. Then he remembered it. Robert Frost! It had obviously just occurred to him because his host's first name was Robert, and then he had pulled another first name out of the air. But who *was* Robert Frost? Suddenly he remembered that too – he was an American poet. Of whom he had never read a syllable. He had hardly read a poem in his whole life, for that matter. God, so that was why this Turner had started talking nonsense about his being a writer!

Robert Turner turned again to his guest. Now tell me what you write.

Nothing special, mumbled his guest.

Robert Turner smiled. A true artist! he said. Have you ever wondered why important artists, especially from Scandinavia – where you obviously come from – have no pride in being what they are? Why they almost feel ashamed of themselves, at least if they haven't created anything that serves a good cause? Art for the downtrodden classes, against nuclear weapons, for women's liberation! If I had been a believing Christian, I should have said they annoy God with their lack of pride, and at the same time I know there's that special Nordic puritanism that's made these unfortunates feel that their existence lacks justification. A puritanism that demands that men work without the slightest joy and by the sweat of their brow to be of use to their fellow-men.

He leaned back a moment and observed the emaciated man, with his head a trifle tilted, as when one studies a painting or a piece of sculpture. Tries to interpret the details and unify them, in order to form an opinion of the work. To pronounce a judgement.

Then he continued: Once more, allow me to guess. Though when I call it guessing, it's actually, I suppose, only an expression of my own kind of missing pride, for it's obviously a matter of thorough analysis, deduction and conclusion. To begin with, one might think you wrote poetry, for you possibly remind one of the portraits that German romantic artists painted of their poet friends – body thin to the point of starvation, skin pale as a TB victim's, eyes with a lustre that might indicate spiritual pain. That you must die soon fits well, too, for lyric poets should always be in the process of dying. But on closer reflection one realizes that the poem – that holding fast of the moment – is not your form of expression. Yesterday evening when you listened to my stories, you see, you betrayed with your eye and with certain little movements that it wasn't the momentary experiences of the individual but human destinies that engrossed you. One might perhaps think that you were a dramatist, but – and here I must ask you to forgive me – on the basis of my appraisal, you have no sense of people's relationships with each other in the confined world, the enclosed space, that a stage creates. I have looked at you when, as if secretly, you observe the people around us, and what seems to interest you isn't so much the interplay and tension between them but rather what you think you can read of the individual's past, present and possibly future in his or her face, carriage and movements. You display, in other words, an interest in destinies and in the individual person's development from phase to phase, and out of that spring the short story and the novel, which are more descriptive and have a vaguer framework than the clearly marked boundaries of the stage. So I feel fairly certain that narrative prose is your form.

I'm right, am I not? added Robert Turner.

Again the guest reddened. Not because he felt himself revealed, which his host of course assumed, but on the contrary because he was being driven further and further away from a disclosure. From what he had longed for all night and all day as a deliverance.

Yesterday, Robert Turner continued without allowing himself to be affected by his guest's reticence, I told you a story while we sat waiting for our bouillabaisse, and today I think it's your turn to shorten the time. You undoubtedly have some tale or other that one might listen to here under the star-studded sky – a tale that would make the tasty *orektika micros* seem still more seductive when it's placed in front of us on the table.

But I can't . . .

Naturally! exclaimed Robert Turner. How thoughtless of me. Why, a work of art is like a dream – it deserts its creator as it is formed in his consciousness, disappears somehow in the grey light of thought. That's a blessing, for how could a person bear throughout life all the beauty and pain that spring from his brow? But at the same time that's a tragedy, for this beauty and pain are exactly what make the artist feel he has a purpose in life. And so he can never be at peace but must keep on creating for ever. For that reason, let me propose instead that you use me as a receiver for the destinies you are now struggling to shape in your imagination – as a metaphorical canvas for your fumbling brush.

The emaciated guest sighed heavily. He felt himself trapped in an endless darkness by a boundless emptiness, and at the same time it was as if this remarkable, peremptory man made feelings, situations and thoughts take form in his consciousness. As if a door were opened to rooms he indeed knew but to which he had never been able to imagine returning . . . and, surprised by his own words, he leaned forward over the table and began slowly to tell a story.

He was ashamed of himself because of it, but he couldn't stop reading about murders and killings in the newspapers. Not about the victims of snipers' bullets or about those left mutilated after terrorist bombs in Belfast or Beirut, but about people who had been shot in their apartment or stabbed in a car and flung into a grove of trees. He read every single word, and he studied the pictures of the scene of the crime and of the dead people closely, while he glanced over at his wife and their two teenage children to see if they realized what he was doing. Usually he leafed back and forth a bit in the paper to divert possible suspicions. It was more difficult for him to conceal this interest when they sat together in their cramped living-room and watched the news on television. If something about murder came on then, he would talk afterwards about what he had grasped of world events, which in reality never concerned him, so that his wife and two children would have something else to think about, if they had noticed how intensely he had leaned forward towards the old TV set when the details of the murder were given.

Robert Turner, who had been sitting the whole time with his wineglass in his hand and studying it with a mixture of reflection and preoccupation, as if what his guest was telling him was actually taking place behind its engraved surface, suddenly drank up, put down his glass and asked: Which he?

The guest looked up, a shade uneasy. The middle-aged man in the story.

Naturally I understand that, said Robert Turner, but doesn't he have a name? Are you asking me to get interested in a nameless person – a kind of anybody? If this anonymity is supposed to cause the kind of identity confusion modern writers are so engrossed in, but which is an illusion, I can only assure you that it's a failure. A work of art is something one looks at, and so there must *be* something to look at, a reality that conforms to the one all around us, not a trivial he. There must be a person of flesh and blood, with an occupation and a place in society, and above all he must be *called* something. Good lord, it's like the artists of our century tossing some lines down on a piece of paper and imagining they've expressed sorrow or longing or violence without grasping that only what is recognizable – re-created nature and the completely reproduced human being – can express such feelings.

The guest's eye wandered and tried to find a mooring among the people who sat at the tables around them. But he wasn't able to see into these people. In a way they weren't alive to him – they were merely puppets who ate and drank and laughed, the way one does at a restaurant. And he felt dimly a protest within him, a protest against the belief that it wouldn't do to gather them all – and himself too – into a nameless mind. But the feeling only brushed through him, like a breath of wind from the sea beyond, followed by doubt and emptiness.

Of course he has a name, he said in a low voice, but it felt somehow so unnatural, so intimate, to use it when I'm sitting here telling the story. It's quite different when I'm writing. . . .

His voice died away. For the first time he had spoken the words when I'm writing and he felt that he had taken one step more that could not be changed or erased. It was simply *said*.

Well, what is he called, then?

Mogens Klint, said the man who called himself Joseph Frost.

Robert Turner sat motionless, as if, expressionless, he were sampling the name, the way a connoisseur lets wine lie on his tongue, raises it towards his palate – still expectant, a shade doubtful – before at last he either swallows it or spits it out. At last he said: Well, it's reasonable for you to choose a name from your own little corner of the world, I suppose, but for that reason it says nothing to me. Besides it has no poetry, no atmosphere, no colour. It just seems grey on grey. But perhaps that has something to do with its meaning.

Its meaning?

Why, yes, its meaning. All names have a meaning, and for a writer that should be an obvious tool. Your own name, Joseph, means for instance May the Lord add one son more! Even to us who don't believe in a supernatural lord at all, it sounds beautiful. . . . But Mogens! What kind of beauty can a name like that convey?

Many men are called that where I come from, said the guest in a barely audible voice, and I've never heard it means anything special.

Well, said Robert Turner, it's your story.

The guest looked down at the table and said: In any case he was called Mogens Klint. He always got up before his wife and two children, and one morning when he went down to fetch the newspaper he stiffened at the sight of a headline announcing that a murder had been committed right there in his neighbourhood. A woman in her late twenties had been stabbed in a little backyard apartment. She had been discovered by a neighbour who had noticed in the night that the outer door was ajar. He thought it was odd for the door not to be closed at that hour, so he had gone in and found her on the floor, spattered with blood and with several deep wounds in her breast. The police doctor thought the wounds had been inflicted with a knife, but the weapon wasn't to be found anywhere, so the murderer must have made off with it. No one could discover any motive either, for nothing seemed to have been removed from the shabby and poorly furnished apartment, and according to what the neighbour said, the victim was never visited by anyone, either men or women. On the other hand, she was three months' pregnant, and possibly that had some connection with the murder, which in the opinion of the police was unusually brutal.

Under the headline there was a picture of the murdered woman, not very clear, probably because it was an enlarged passport photo. A not noticeably beautiful but almost touchingly innocent face surrounded by medium-length hair. It struck Mogens Klint that she seemed considerably younger than the age given, but obviously that could be because the picture had been taken several years before, and he thought that maybe she had been a woman no one had wanted to photograph. There was also a picture of the apartment building, and he recognized it at once, because he usually bought cigarettes in a tobacco shop that was right beside the gateway into the backyard.

During breakfast with his wife and two children Mogens Klint pretended he hadn't even noticed the report of the murder and merely made some vague remarks when his wife and children began to talk about something like that really happening just around the corner from where they lived. It irritated him, quite simply, that they became so taken up with something that was no business of theirs, as if they were noisily forcing their way into a territory he felt was his own. Particularly the children's comments on the picture of the murdered woman, and their speculations about whether she was raped before she was stabbed, actually made him ill, and at last he just got up from the kitchen table and walked out of the house without preparing a lunch-pack and without saying goodbye – something, for that matter, he seldom or never said. His wife and children had in fact long ago stopped noticing when he came and went.

Except when it was really cold in the winter he usually walked to the little shipping firm out in Amager where he had worked for most of his life. That morning, almost without thinking about it, he took the route along the street where the young woman had lived and entered the tobacco shop. After buying a packet of cigarettes, he asked for all the morning papers, and when the little old tobacco lady took his money, she began talking about the murder. Mogens Klint suddenly felt that he couldn't endure the little tobacconist – the sharp, wrinkled face shone with a greed that filled him with disgust. Nevertheless he listened, for the old woman, who had a small apartment behind the tobacco shop, could give him details of which the journalists as yet had no knowledge. Above all, about the murdered woman. It turned out that the young woman had been without work for a long time, apparently because she had been ill. The tobacco lady didn't know exactly what had been wrong with her, but thought it had been something to do with her chest. In any case she had often stayed in bed all day, so the tobacco lady herself had had to see that she got food, and finally there had been so little money that the old woman had had to spend her own. But she had written it down in a book – every last penny.

Mogens Klint remembered reading that the murdered woman had never been visited by anyone, and he asked as casually as he could if she hadn't had men or women friends who could have taken care of her. Then he thought that the wrinkled face became still sharper, and that the eyes shone still more greedily than before. First she pressed her mouth tightly together into a razor-thin line, then she bent forward over the counter and said in a low voice that there had been *one* person who came to her now and then late of an evening. She had never seen anything, just heard the footsteps and the door of her apartment opening and closing, but she was quite sure it had been a man. Had mentioned it to her, at which she had blushed, but hadn't said a word. But now of course it had come out that she had been expecting a child. What more did you need to know? When Mogens Klint asked the tobacco lady if she had told any of this to the police, she said she hadn't. Because they hadn't asked. For the most part they had questioned only some young people who lived in the apartment directly opposite the murdered woman. As if *they* knew something just because they were young. Her, why, they'd scarcely given her a minute, and it wasn't any of her business, anyway, to meddle in police work.

When Mogens Klint arrived at the small shipping office in Amager, a few minutes late for the first time in his life, it was difficult for him to work. As soon as he felt certain that the others were busy, he took out the newspapers and read carefully what they said about the murder, even what he had read on the stairs at home. Finally he cut out the pictures of the young woman, which were all different enlargements of the passport photo, folded them up and put them in his wallet. Then he threw the papers into the waste-paper basket. But it was still difficult for him to concentrate on his work. Each time he tried to add up the long columns of figures, he saw before him the murdered woman's face. Frankly, it was fairly expressionless and revealed nothing of what she might have felt or thought when the picture was taken, but little by little he could dimly detect a weak smile, as if a shadow of recognition glided over the small, slightly narrow mouth, and he fancied that her eye sought his, asked him for something.

After a while he could see her body in front of him too, which of course wasn't shown in any of the pictures – frail and helpless, with hands like a child's. He pictured to himself how she had lain on the floor in that wretched apartment, with wide-open eyes, while the blood spurted out over her white blouse. Whether her blouse – if that's what she had been wearing – had actually been white, he naturally had no idea. He was just certain that it must have been. As certain as he was that at the sight of the knife she had drawn her legs up against her stomach and held out those slender hands towards him helplessly. As if to defend herself? To receive him? Curiously enough, without its frightening him for a moment, it gave him a strange feeling of superiority and power to see her lying like that with a cautiously wavering, beseeching smile, while she stammered out something in a low voice, incoherently. What was it she was trying to say?

On his way home from work Mogens Klint reached the tobacco shop just as the old tobacco lady was going to close it up. He had made no conscious decision what he would do, but when he stood at the counter it suddenly felt quite natural for him to say that he was actually from the police, and that he wanted to see the murdered woman's apartment once more. Unfortunately he had forgotten the key, he said, but he knew of course that the tobacconist had taken care of the sick young woman and that she must therefore have one. The old woman stiffened and again her mouth became a razor-thin line. He knew that a struggle was taking place inside her, a struggle between her resentment about being deceived and a kind of greedy delight at being asked – at someone's finally understanding that she was the one who really knew something. At last she locked the door of the shop and indicated to Mogens Klint that he should follow her into something he had thought was a back room to the shop but which proved to be a dirty little apartment. The key lay in a jar on top of a cupboard. She didn't give it to him but put it into her apron pocket and walked in front of him out into the backyard, over to the murdered woman's apartment.

Mogens Klint knew that she wanted to stay inside with him, so he said it was against regulations for outsiders to enter the apartment. Again he saw resentment in that sharp face, but she gave him the key, hesitantly, as if she knew she wouldn't get it back. Then she turned round and went back to her own place without a word.

The murdered woman's apartment was about as he had imagined it. A small hallway, where she had been found, a kitchen and a sitting-room that was also used as a bedroom. The few tawdry pieces of furniture looked as if they had come from different places. She had probably brought most of them with her from home and had perhaps bought some second-hand. A divan had been made up for the night, but she was unlikely to have lain on it before she was killed, for a cheap, light-blue nightdress lay neatly folded on the pillow.

He sat down on the divan, on the very edge, as if she lay there in reality with the same wavering, beseeching smile as he had earlier imagined. She wasn't used to making decisions about herself – about anything at all, really. For she was nothing, she felt, so how could she then have any right to make decisions? Mogens Klint felt that she was looking at him, vacillating between fright and hope, as if he were destiny itself. Again he had the strange feeling of superiority and power – strange because otherwise he never felt anything like that. He knew he could do what he wanted with her, and calmly, almost matter of factly, he took off her the light-blue nightdress. She made no resistance, and it was impossible for him to tell by her face if it was the first time she had let a man undress her. Though he knew, of course, that she must have done. It was also impossible to know if she really understood what was going to happen, if she realized that he was going to lie with her. The wavering, beseeching eyes certainly betrayed that she was frightened, but they told nothing about what she feared. It was more a fear of something she couldn't identify. Something unknown. For a moment, but only for a moment, he was touched by the sight of that frail body and of skin as white as if it had never been in the sun. As if she had never ventured out on a beach, still less lain by the shore on a slope of naked rock.

So he imagined that he lay with her, and everything was more real than he had ever experienced before. She did nothing, simply complied with his wishes, and not a movement suggested that she felt anything, either desire or despair. It was merely something that happened to her, the way everything else happened without her quite understanding why, and again he was touched for a moment, this time by her helpless innocence. Sometimes it seemed as if she thought – if one could call it thinking – that she ought to come towards him, ought to try taking within her something she sensed from afar as what one means by nearness, and as a hint of this he noticed that her hands needed to touch his skin. But none of this hindered him, nothing interfered with his experience of ruling over another person, almost over life and death. He thought: The man in me has created her. I can let her live or I can kill her, and she'll let my will be done regardless! But at the same time he felt a terrifying emptiness. Like a call without a reply.

Afterwards he got up and looked round the little sitting-room. Stood looking at something ridiculous, some small porcelain figures on a little crooked bookcase, some kind of dog and puppies, and as if distractedly he put one of the puppies in his jacket pocket. Some old weekly magazines were lying at the bottom of the bookcase, and above them stood a handful of books, probably from her childhood. He took out one of them and leafed through it, and suddenly discovered a letter between the pages.

At first he thought it was to her, but there was nothing on the outside of the envelope, and when he opened it and read the letter he realized that she had written it herself, possibly to the man the little tobacco lady had spoken of. It, too, was helpless, with clumsy, uneven letters and a lot of space between the words, as if she wasn't used to writing letters. In place of a date there was just a day of the week, and there was really no heading – it just began Dear friend. Perhaps she hadn't been sure what his name was or how it was spelled. He expected it to say something about her being pregnant, for after all the papers had said that she was three months' gone, but there was nothing but some cautious sentences about her hoping that he would come back some time. At the bottom she had merely written her name, her last name too, as though she hadn't felt confident he would remember her if she had just used her first name. It struck Mogens Klint that she possibly hadn't known she was going to have a child, that maybe she hadn't even quite realized how one does. Once more he was touched, and at the same time he felt as if his body was growing to superhuman size. He could, you might say, let the little woman lie in his hand and close his fingers around her naked form.

After reading the letter several times he placed it between the pages of the book and was going to put it back on the shelf. Then he noticed that her pen was also lying in the bookcase, and he slowly took the letter out again. Then he wrote in a clumsy, uneven hand his own name and the address of the shipping firm in Amager on the outside of the envelope, sealed it and stuck on a stamp that lay in a bowl beside the small porcelain figures. After that, he wrote her name and address as sender. It is difficult to say whether he quite realized what he was doing. Whether he was quite conscious of it, or whether it took place as in a trance or in a dream. On the way home he put the letter in the first post-box he came to, and when, immediately afterwards, he saw a telephone kiosk, he went in calmly, dialled the number for the police and told them that he knew who had killed the young woman and that she had written a letter to the murderer just before she was killed. That's all he said, and when he was asked who was ringing, he just put the receiver down.

Robert Turner raised his eyebrows. Good lord, he exclaimed, was the man mad?

No, said his guest hesitantly, hardly mad. Merely relieved.

Relieved?

Yes, I think he was. Though maybe it would be more accurate to say that Mogens Klint didn't quite know *what* he felt, only that he had intervened in something. Had acted. When he finally came home, he gave neither his wife nor his children so much as a glance but walked straight into his bedroom, lay down and fell almost immediately into a deep and dreamless sleep.

But he woke up early, even before daybreak, got up and left without waiting for his wife and children to do so. Anyway, they would hardly notice that he was gone, for the children had long since stopped saying good morning to him and he could no longer remember when his wife had last said anything to him or stroked his cheek when she opened her eyes. The only way he knew they were aware of his existence was that they didn't bump into him when they had to pass each other in the hall or in the kitchen.

The old tobacco lady still hadn't opened her shop and he didn't knock on the door of her apartment, but walked straight into the depressing backyard. In reality he was standing there even before he was conscious why. But there are so many different levels of consciousness, and maybe the reason he found himself in this backyard was that ever since he had read about the murder he had tried to imagine, in one of the out-of-the-way places of his mind, what had become of the knife she had been stabbed with. The police had naturally searched her apartment, overturned rubbish bins and rummaged in each of the many piles of garbage that lay along the walls in the backyard – without success. So probably it wasn't unreasonable to think that the murderer had taken the knife with him. But Mogens Klint couldn't quite picture the murderer doing that, and besides, when he had come from the murdered woman's apartment the evening before, he had a strange feeling of what the murderer had done. To begin with it had been so vague that he hadn't attached any importance to it, but gradually it had become more and more distinct. The separate parts of the feeling had begun to take form like pieces of a puzzle – a man in a state of panic, a quick movement of a hand, a rusty drainpipe from a gutter. When he woke up in the morning he saw the whole thing before him in a flash. Yet it was like something he had dreamed, and it was still unclear to him whether the rusty drainpipe actually ran down the wall by the door where he thought he had seen it.

But it did. For a moment Mogens Klint stood there, as if to give the feeling time to rise up into the clear light of day, so he could be sure that it hadn't been a dream. Then he walked calmly over to the drainpipe. It was an old pipe, corroded by rust and burst to pieces by winter ice, so that there was a comparatively long crack on the part at the back. It was impossible to see through the crack, for it was pressed between the pipe and the wall, but by bending the rusty metal he managed to widen the opening enough to get two fingers into the pipe. Then he felt something that he knew must be the knife, and very carefully he wormed it out.

Because half-consciously he had been convinced that the murder weapon lay hidden in the drainpipe, he didn't become elated, as he would have done if he had discovered it by accident, but standing there with the knife in his hand filled him with a feeling he had never known before. He saw again in front of him the young woman lying on the floor in the shabby apartment, but this time he felt not only superiority and power but something that suggested unrestrained hatred. It was as if he shouted at her. Who did she think she was, she who thought she could save her life with a few faint, seemingly innocent smiles and incoherent words? Merely by letting herself be used, one night, as a dumb and passive animal? Why did she never stroke his cheek any more when she woke up in the morning, or come to him with a lust that made him feel like a man?

Trembling with indignation, Mogens Klint put the knife, which had reddish-brown stains of congealed blood on both blade and handle, into his inside pocket. She had got what she deserved – had learned you can't, unpunished, convert a man into an inescapable destiny. . . . Innocence! He smiled to himself. Now at least she had realized, even if just in a painful flash, that it's no use pretending not to understand.

When Mogens Klint arrived at the little shipping firm in Amager – late that morning too – there was no letter on his desk. First he became uneasy, but then he thought that it would arrive by a later post. Letters put in the box in the evening didn't always arrive early the next morning. As if to assure himself that everything was as it should be, he put his hand inside his jacket and felt to see if the knife was in his pocket. It was, and his whole body seemed to calm down when his fingers touched the cold knife blade. But he was unable to get down to work. The long columns of figures seemed to him fairly unimportant, and he slowly turned towards the window.

After he had been sitting like that for a while, looking out at the roofs of houses and at the grey sky, a man with a brief-case came unobtrusively through the door. Although Mogens Klint had imagined it quite differently, above all not so calm and undramatic, he knew at once that the man was from the police. He thought he should stand up, but before he got that far the policeman had sat down directly opposite him and almost apologetically placed a police badge on the desk. Then he took the letter from his brief-case and gave it to Mogens Klint. I'm sorry we had to open it, he said, but I'm sure you'll understand why. Your boss happened to notice that the sender was the girl who was murdered and he rang us up. Would you mind telling me why it's addressed to you?

While Mogens Klint pretended to read the letter, he tried to think. True enough he hadn't visualized his arrest as a dramatic struggle, a muster of policemen and cars with sirens, but this unassuming-looking man transformed it all into something almost humiliatingly commonplace. An outsider would never have dreamt that the conversation actually concerned the investigation of a girl's murder. After he had placed the letter in the post-box, it was the confession itself that he had thought through most carefully. It would take place in his boss's office with the other employees standing terror stricken outside the door. Sometimes he also thought that his wife would be summoned and that she would sit looking at him, conscience stricken and terrified that she had never known who he was. Expressionless and silent he would stand for a long time looking at them all, before at last saying that there was hardly any point in denying it, now that the letter had exposed him. But everything had turned out so differently from what he had imagined. Therefore he said clumsily, almost without being conscious of it: Shall I come with you now?

Why? asked the policeman gently.

Because I was the one who killed her, said Mogens Klint, and as if to emphasize his words he took the knife from his inside jacket pocket and laid it in front of him on the desk. But it could have been any knife at all. The policeman in fact cast only a glance at it before he placed it in a transparent plastic bag he had in his brief-case.

Where did you find it?

Find it! said Mogens Klint. I took it with me after I'd stabbed her. You know I did, because you searched everywhere and couldn't find it.

The policeman looked straight ahead thoughtfully. But now we know it was in the drainpipe, he said quietly. The murderer has confessed he hid it there. Besides, we knew the pipe had been bent out this morning because it wasn't when we were there yesterday evening, and so you must have gone and got it just now on your way here. Not so stupid of you, thinking of that hiding-place. We should have done so too.

The murderer? cried Mogens Klint, but he felt that his voice was failing and that he was close to losing his grip. But didn't you hear me say *I* killed her? Why, you came here because of the letter she sent me. Would you have done so if it hadn't proved I was involved with her?

The policeman's voice became still gentler, as if it actually pained him to say what he was compelled to. He could scarcely restrain himself from putting his hand on Mogens Klint's arm. You probably didn't even know who she was, he said. If you look closely at the letter, you'll notice something odd. It was posted almost a day after the girl had been murdered. They say all criminals make at least one mistake, and that holds good too, I suppose, for people who want to give the impression they are. Apart from that, the writing on the envelope seems at first to be the same as that on the writing-paper itself, but if you study it carefully you'll see it's only a clumsy imitation. The tobacconist has told us you were in the murdered girl's apartment yesterday afternoon, and we think you found this letter and posted it to yourself. You needn't tell me why you did, but I think you ought to know that the real murderer – who we caught last night – is a brutal man who uses people. You don't seem to be like that, and you should be glad.

Then the policeman got up, took his brief-case and walked towards the door. When he was about to close it after him, he stood there for a moment looking at the thin form that sat slumped over the desk. It would have been better, he thought, if he could have taken him with him. I mentioned to your boss, he said, that this conversation might be a shock to you and that you should have the day off because of that. You must naturally decide for yourself if you'd rather try to work, but it would probably be the best thing if you went home to your family. . . . You can keep the letter, by the way. After all, it *was* in a way to you.

But Mogens Klint didn't move.

The man who called himself Joseph Frost didn't move either, but sat there almost without breathing. For the first time in his life he had told a story, and he felt naked and empty. Scraped out. As if Robert Turner had removed a secret foetus in him with his eating utensils and sat examining it on the plate in front of him. Dissecting it carefully with his knife and fork and regarding the cut-up organs with a coolly appraising eye. What is it the professor sees, he thought, that I haven't seen myself? Is there something he understands that I should have understood and that has now been irrevocably revealed? It was only a story anyway.

Robert Turner sipped the local Greek wine, and when the guest tried to catch his eye, as if to get an answer to his unspoken question, he found him preoccupied, suggesting that his host's entire attention was concentrated on the wine's distinctive taste. When Robert Turner finally put down his glass, he said: Well, perhaps you'll make something of your story, if you actually write it down some time, but as it is, I'm inclined to think that it lengthened our waiting time rather than shortened it. Seeing that we have our little agreement about frankness, I assume you won't mind my saying that you have a discouraging love of the trivial and the ugly. Tragedy, naturally, belongs to literary composition, but you must spare your readers this dirty-grey banality that never lifts the characters on to the tragic plane. Take for example the young woman in your story. Three months' pregnant! Is it to satisfy your social conscience that you introduce such homespun trifles? Besides, since she has such limited appeal — from your description of her — surely it's almost unthinkable that anyone would have got her into such a condition. . . . And what does she have in her bookcase? The Greek tragedies, Byron, or at any rate *The Four Quartets* by that American, T.S. Eliot? No, a handful of children's books that perhaps she wasn't even able to read but just used as a hiding-place for clumsy, unsent letters! How can such a character cast a revealing light into our minds and uplift us? The only possible uplift is that at least you kill her off.

The thin guest looked down. Maybe she was like that, he mumbled.

Like that! Robert Turner rolled his eyes and was going to say something else, but he paused, for the first course was then being placed on the table. With extreme care, as if he were not at all certain of the result, he sampled a morsel and after a short while nodded appreciatively but curtly to the young waiter, who then retired. Then he put his fork down and said: Frost, my dear fellow, I have said, to be sure, that art must be a rendering of reality. But not of just *any* reality. Not of banalities. An artist must *choose* among the many realities. Some author or other is supposed to have said that writing is finding a story for one's experience – but what if the writer's experiences are only grey trivialities? Something must be added to reality before it takes off and lets us feel what flight is like up there among the Muses. Take, for example, this first course – which, thank God, has at last arrived. Are there black prawns squirming about on the plate? No, they've been re-created! Our friend Haralambos, the chef, has with his magic saucepans given them a pink glow, exalted them in golden oil and sprinkled them with lemon juice, which – with its touch of bitterness – sharpens our senses, opening them to the divine experience that conceals itself behind the prawns' black shells. In short, let us enjoy the artist's *orektika micros*!

They ate in silence, the host slowly, as if each mouthful were a revelation, the guest considerably faster. To tell the truth, the guest experienced neither the exalted nor the divine, and by the time he had emptied his plate it is quite possible that he couldn't tell what he had eaten. As he sat waiting for Robert Turner to finish, he was really only conscious of a conflicting mixture of shame and defiance. . . . But what if one's experiences *are* just grey trivialities? he asked himself. Could one reality be more valid than another? Did these damned prawns assume more distinction, seen as reality, because they had been cooked in oil and sprinkled with lemon juice? Were his experiences less valuable than those his host had harvested in French hunting lodges, among famous artists and at the world's universities? He had no answer, for he had nothing but his own experiences. Though hadn't Robert Turner said only the previous evening that all people were interesting?

He looked up at his host, and in a flash he hated this person who sat there enjoying the last little prawn. As keenly as he enjoys himself, the guest thought, and felt at the same instant a blush of shame at having such thoughts about a man who not only had generously allowed him to sit at his table but had shown trust in him.

When Robert Turner had wiped his mouth carefully with his napkin and given a sign to the waiter, the thin guest bent towards him and said: That child you were telling me about yesterday evening, the one you first met at your own grave – I've been thinking a lot about her. She was called Eurydice, wasn't she? ... Also about what you said about having been dead.

He felt his cheeks grow warm on account of the awkward way he had expressed himself, as if, from humility, he hadn't dared ask directly to be told more about this strange child who had obviously meant so much to his host. But his shame at having felt a flash of hatred towards this man still overwhelmed him.

Robert Turner put down his napkin. Eurydice was just one of the many names I called her, he said. What her real name was, is of no consequence. I'm not even certain if I remember it. From your vague comment, I gather you'd like to hear more about her, and in the light of our agreement of utter frankness I shall naturally respond. Later. Your story about this – I'm sorry to say – rather uninteresting woman was unexpectedly long, you know, and so the main course is already on its way before the taste of those admirable prawns has left one's palate. It's unfortunate, but the lamb must be eaten now while it's freshly cooked.

The guest felt the flush in his cheeks still more strongly, not so much because of shame over his flash of hatred, but because he felt guilty of having ruined the dinner with that long story of his, and because he couldn't quite understand the things Robert Turner had said. He was alarmed by those long-winded and at the same time well-formulated sentences, by all the words that seemed so elusive and difficult, perhaps without being so. As if the professor were putting him in his place. He had been stupid, for obviously a child couldn't be called Eurydice, but nevertheless there was surely no reason for talking to him like that.

This time both the head waiter and the young waiter came, and it was the head waiter who served. Suddenly Robert Turner's face became quite rigid and his eyes grew narrow, almost invisible. With the point of his knife, as if to avoid any contact with it, he took a piece of meat from his plate and held it up before the head waiter, and in the light from the small table-lamp there was the suspicion of a yellowish white streak in the dark flesh.

Is this supposed to be lean?

Robert Turner rose so abruptly that his chair overturned, but he ignored it, just forced his way out quickly between the tables. Without even once turning round, he walked along the quay until at last he disappeared behind the walls of the Crusaders' old castle. Not till then did his emaciated guest rise and mumble something disjointed to the head waiter about their probably returning the next evening.

Then he walked to his hotel.

THE THIRD
EVENING

THE emaciated man who called himself Joseph Frost was uneasy all the next day owing to Robert Turner's unexpectedly strong, almost theatrical reaction to the strip of fat in the lamb, and he walked early to the restaurant where they had eaten together the past two evenings. He grew no less uneasy when he saw that Robert Turner wasn't sitting at any of the small tables under the plane and carob trees beside the pavement, and hesitantly sank down at the table where they had sat the evening before. When the head waiter came almost immediately with the menu, he said in a somewhat helpless stammer that he didn't want to order until the professor arrived, and the head waiter beckoned expressionlessly to the young waiter, who placed a glass of water in front of him on the table with almost demonstrative carelessness. They had not, of course, forgotten the lamb episode.

But it wasn't just Robert Turner's peculiar behaviour that made him uneasy. That morning, in fact, a letter from his wife had arrived, and he couldn't remember ever receiving one before. True enough, he himself wrote often, occasionally almost every day, but he never received a reply. He didn't expect one either, for actually she wasn't the one to whom he wrote. That is to say he naturally put her name at the top of the sheet, and he thought it was her he had in his thoughts as he wrote, but it was at any rate not her as she was now. Maybe she simply had never been the person of whom he was thinking, as he sat under the evening sky at the table out on the balcony. Smiling, he pictured to himself how she would laugh at his descriptions of the noisy tourists or be moved by his portrayals of frightened, ragged children who tried to sell him withered flowers to earn a few wretched drachmas, but both the laughter and the compassionate eyes belonged to a woman he had in fact never seen. Nevertheless, when he put his pen down for a moment, he imagined he saw her in front of him as she had stood with the two children and waved to him at Kastrup Airport. To begin with he had been uncertain, but gradually he could somehow see her more and more clearly, and the strange thing was that she grew younger at the same time. Or maybe it was just that her eyes grew more and more radiant, exactly as they had been that first time she had really looked at him. Then he picked up his pen again and went on writing.

When he came down to breakfast at the hotel that morning and discovered the letter in the little pigeon-hole over his room number – which always used to be empty – he became confused, but also thought that he saw those radiant eyes more clearly in front of him than ever before. He reached out for the letter, and suddenly, just as he touched the outside of the envelope and could see the writing, the radiant eyes vanished from in front of him. It was as if they had never existed. And he just stood there looking at the letter and thinking that it must be for someone else. Though his reason told him that it was crazy, he said to himself that, after all, he was Joseph Frost and that therefore he had no right to read a letter to a stranger.

For a while immediately after that he saw himself from the outside, as if he were a casual spectator in one of the dark corners of the hotel lobby. He saw a lean, middle-aged man walk slowly over to a writing-table in the quietest part of the lobby. There he remained standing for a time, and it could be that he was trying to think. Then he bent down, pulled out a waste-paper basket that stood under the table and carefully tore the letter into tiny pieces, which fluttered into the basket.

Perhaps because all his attention was focused on the downward fluttering pieces of paper he could still see quite clearly in front of him, he didn't notice Robert Turner until he stood right beside the table. Reddening, he tried to get up so that the slightly older man wouldn't consider him impolite, but he was sitting in such a constricted position that he could make only a clumsy movement, which almost upset the small table.

Robert Turner appeared to be in excellent humour. He greeted the head waiter effusively and said that during his entire stroll through the town down to the harbour he had been picturing to himself various interesting dishes that could make a radiant day still more radiant, but that he still hadn't quite made up his mind because he wanted to describe the alternatives to his young friend.

The guest reddened again, for he wasn't young in any case – was hardly much younger than Robert Turner – but, fearful that his host would be annoyed and lose some of his good humour, he didn't dare protest. Instead he asked, as if to encourage his host to explain why this particular day had been so radiant: Have you found her?

Robert Turner looked wonderingly at him. Whom should I have found?

The child, said the guest. You told me, you know, that you had come here to look for the girl you met in the churchyard, and I thought that you had actually found her, since you're so happy.

Oh, the child, said Robert Turner. No, I haven't found her. But I look for her every day – search for her in both the most likely and the most unlikely places – and I know that one day I'll suddenly spot her. This morning I even walked into every blessed corner of the dig they're doing of the ancient town that once existed here, for I remember how attentively she listened to my little improvised talks on classical art and architecture. She was especially moved when I told her about sculptors like Praxiteles, Lysippus and Phidias. As you undoubtedly remember, there were artists distinguished by the ability to let the typical and the individual achieve complete equilibrium, at the same time as they – especially Phidias –

let their marvellous sculptures show how the very body and its movements, and not primarily the face, can express human feelings.

But she wasn't there?

No, she wasn't, Robert Turner said and sat down at the table with an air that informed his guest how silly it was to ask questions that have already been answered and that, besides, the time had now come to study the menu. Although in fact the study of the menu was only a superficial gesture – a quick survey, really, to assure oneself that a tasty meal could be produced only after the head waiter had been given careful instructions as to what kind of food one wanted and how it should be prepared.

Robert Turner had long since given clear expression to the view that during the planning of a meal one must never let oneself be distracted by irrelevant chatter. Nevertheless he asked, perhaps to demonstrate how superfluous he thought it was to spend time on such a litany of culinary banalities, but without taking his eye from the bill of fare, from what kind of illness his guest feared he was dying.

Courths-Mahler's Disease, the guest mumbled.

Robert Turner leaned back and with closed eyes he repeated to himself thoughtfully in a low voice what the guest had said. It was clear he had never heard of the disease but that the name itself said something to him without his being able to think what. It annoyed him, for he couldn't bear to be reminded of his age by feeling that his memory was failing. He just hoped fervently that this idiotic problem wouldn't ruin his meal for him. In order to avoid such a potential catastrophe, he put down the bill of fare and asked: How does this Courths-Mahler's Disease develop, then?

The guest had feared this question, which of course he knew had to come, for he hadn't a clue why precisely this name had occurred to him when Robert Turner had asked him about his illness. Hoping somehow that the slightly older man wouldn't then pursue the question, he said in a low voice that it was the kind of disease one prefers not to talk about.

Robert Turner smiled. But my dear chap, he said, in the first place we have our agreement about utter frankness, and in the second we are experienced men who know about most things in life, who know indeed that the lust of the flesh sometimes leads to the destruction of the body. I've seen especially among my artist friends how a wild life in youth has led to an early death in the madhouse. I was once shown a brain that had belonged to one of our most gifted illustrators who unfortunately ended his days like this, and it had become as smooth as a plum and so shrunken that it could have lain in a child's hand. Naturally I can't disclose his name to you – can merely say that he was quite close to me at one period. But your illness hasn't progressed so far in any case, for, from what I can judge, your sanity is still intact.

I think so, said the guest in a low voice.

It's interesting, by the way, Robert Turner continued, that while to begin with I knew I had heard the name of your illness but was unable to recall in what connection, it suddenly dawned on me during our conversation just now that there was once a German writer called Hedwig Courths-Mahler who wrote rather unimportant novels about trivial, sentimental love. It would undoubtedly have been an amusing whim of fate if, for instance, her brother or her son was the doctor who gave his name to the disease you suffer from.

Once again the guest reddened. Not because Robert Turner had so intimately described the very tragic course of the illness from which he obviously believed his guest suffered, but because he was afraid that Robert Turner actually understood that there was no such thing as Courths-Mahler's Disease. That he had just pulled the name out of the air. Or, more correctly, that it had bobbed to the surface of his consciousness as a distant memory of a book, probably one in a bookcase at the home of an old aunt with a weakness for sentimental novels. Again in the hope of saving a desperate situation, he said, in a low voice and with a carefully calculated side glance at the guests at the other tables: Courths-Mahler's Disease doesn't affect the brain.

What does it affect, then? asked Robert Turner.

The heart, the guest whispered, still with the vague backing of his aunt's modest bookcase. But that only happens after many years, for the disease becomes encapsulated and just lies there as a hidden poison in the body. . . . At any rate, that was how the doctors explained it to me, he added uncertainly.

And soon you'll die, then?

Yes, said his guest.

Death was an occurrence that Robert Turner didn't consider worth mentioning. He had mentioned earlier, after all, that he himself had experienced it physically and that people's anxieties about it were, in his opinion, greatly exaggerated. Therefore he turned without so much as a sympathetic nod back to the real problem – namely, which interesting dishes would make the forthcoming meal a perfect ending to a radiant day. Not for a moment did it occur to Robert Turner that this, in his judgement, rather uncultivated guest would be capable of offering advice in matters of a culinary nature, and if, contrary to his presumption, that actually happened, he naturally wouldn't have dreamed of taking any notice of it. But simply because he liked to think aloud, he leaned back in his chair all the same and asked pleasantly: What do you think about a *fakes soupa* to begin with? It's still quite hot, you know, what with the sun roasting away all day. Don't you think too that a soup like that's the very thing that might refresh us?

The guest nodded cautiously.

As you surely remember, continued Robert Turner without letting himself be affected by his guest's uncertainty, *fakes soupa* is made from the seeds of *Lens esculenta*. This splendid member of the pea family was probably imported from the Orient in antiquity and, especially in Lent, it saves many people down here from needlessly going hungry. The question is merely whether the kitchen staff have had lentils soaking in cold water overnight, and whether the tomatoes that must be mashed and added to the soup just before it has boiled are fresh enough. I assume you agree with me that otherwise it will have a rather insipid taste?

Afterwards, said Robert Turner before his guest had said anything at all, when it's a trifle cooler, I wouldn't mind a *moshari vrasto*. It's a boiled dish too, of course, but the veal is fished out of the pot, you know, and cut into thin slices and placed on a warm dish before it's served with courgettes, noodles and other delicacies. How does that sound?

This time the guest didn't answer either, something to which neither of them seemed to give so much as a thought, though perhaps they felt a certain relief, for Robert Turner turned immediately to the head waiter, who had appeared unnoticed and stood ready with pad and pencil. The guest noted that Robert Turner's eyes grew narrow during the ordering, and he realized that they *hadn't* had lentils soaking overnight in cold water. The head waiter maintained that this was a problem which could be solved very easily, for he could obtain lentils from his cousin who ran a restaurant in the vicinity, where they always had lentils soaking for the preparation of *fakes soupa*. Robert Turner put his hands on the arm-rests of his chair, as if to get up and leave, but perhaps the thought of the previous evening caused him to restrain himself, for he remained seated all the same and said, even if rather coolly, that provided the tomatoes were absolutely fresh, he wouldn't let this ruin an otherwise radiant day.

Then he turned calmly to his guest. You mentioned the child, he said, and seeing that we must wait for the lentil soup anyhow, as our friend the head waiter still seems to have something to learn about running a first-class restaurant, I may perhaps be allowed to shorten the time for you by telling you how my strange little goddess of destiny led to a change in my life that very few people are privileged to experience.

When, one afternoon, quite outside the routine of my Sunday trips, I walked to the churchyard to gain peace of mind by letting my eyes rest upon the beautiful statue of the nude young girl I had erected, I discovered that there was a person kneeling and tending the flowers on *my* grave. At first I supposed it was some churchyard gardener who thought that the grave wasn't tidy enough, and I became very indignant, for it was scarcely a week since I had weeded it and I had even planted a little rose-bush there. It didn't improve matters that I, as I have mentioned, had gone there precisely to gain peace of mind after a harrowing clash at the university with a student who interrupted me in the middle of a lecture on Constable.

As you undoubtedly know, John Constable was one of our most distinguished painters, and my lecture was – I think I may venture to say – both inspiring and marked by my unreserved admiration for his poetic feeling for landscape. I was just going to stress his indebtedness to both the Dutch masters and the Venetians when this student suddenly shouted that such idyll painters had been harmful to society by diverting people's thoughts from the injustice and oppression that followed in the wake of the Industrial Revolution! I couldn't believe my ears. One must possibly tolerate the lack of refinement he clearly displayed in interrupting his professor in the middle of a lecture, and I did so too, I trust, seeing that young people today haven't a clue what refinement means. But it appalled me that a person who intended to dedicate his life to the study of art, vulgarized art to such an extent and demanded of artists that they turn their eyes away from the universe and down into the muddy aquarium that one's times always are.

At first I naturally ignored him and continued to point out Constable's lush and living colours and his ability to reproduce reality exactly as it is. But the student wouldn't give in – just shouted louder and louder and asked which reality I was talking about, the child labourers' or their lordships'! Masterfully, but with complete self-control, I answered that whether one was a child in a mine or a duke in his castle, nature would always be an expression of the earth's eternal beauty, and that both high and low could have their minds enriched by the strong insight into nature's wonderful mysteries that a painter like Constable created with his pictures. Then others began to shout too and a few even laughed.

At you? the guest asked.

Robert Turner shrugged his shoulders. No one can protect himself against the laughter of fools, he said. But enough of that. It was only to explain to you why I needed the churchyard's blessed peace, and why I became still more indignant than perhaps I would have become otherwise over the fact that someone, if I may say so, was trampling about in my peace-filled circles. When I came closer I saw, however, that it was the child, my Eurydice, who was kneeling there and carefully removing a few dried-up leaves and some withered snapdragons. Quietly I sat down on the bench in front of the grave, and remained there looking at her with emotion. At her face, which radiated a rare tenderness despite its coarse features, at her hands, which touched the plants so carefully, as if they were young birds, and at her youthful form – innocent and at the same time so strong. After a while she turned slowly and smiled at me calmly, as if she had known the whole time that I was sitting there. As if it were a matter of course that we were together – that in a way we always were and therefore didn't need to say hello or tell unimportant things to each other.

Then she rose and came over to me. Don't you think she's pleased now? she asked.

Who?

Your daughter. . . . After a while, cautiously: How old was she?

Only a few years older than you.

The answer came quite of itself, for I couldn't think it over, you know. It would have seemed very peculiar if I couldn't have said straight away how old my daughter was when she died, and naturally I had completely forgotten that I had told her it was my daughter lying there, because I couldn't very well have disclosed that, pending the arrival of my own lifeless body, the grave was simply empty. To the question of how old this daughter of mine was I therefore hadn't given a thought, but – basically – about fifteen wasn't at all a bad age for a dead daughter.

It began to get dark, and it struck me a trifle uneasily that this child oughtn't to be in a churchyard so late. You mustn't misunderstand me. I have no notions about the dead rising from their graves or about people not staying in such a place after dark for other reasons. But I thought that a child after all is a child, perhaps with fantasies of just that kind, and that her family might possibly grow worried about her as well. So I said: It was touching of you to tend my daughter's grave, and I'm certain she's pleased now, as you put it – but shouldn't you go home now before it gets too dark?

She looked at me, and again she smiled. Home with you?

What happened then I hardly understood myself, so I don't expect you to do so, but it dawned on me that this was what I had longed for ever since I first met her. The thought of showing her that beautiful little estate, the park which, with its old trees and its idyllic ponds with their profusion of water-lilies, had hardly its equal in all England, and my modest art collection – which none the less contained works by our finest artists – filled me with an indescribable joy. It wasn't because I wanted to impress that innocent child, but because I felt that she was the very person with whom I could share my dearest possession, the one that even more than my work had become myself. Perhaps it sounds neurotic, but every time I came home from the university or from one of my many travels, I would notice how my heart almost stood still until I saw that my palatial house wasn't burned down and that the park hadn't been devastated by a storm. I often thought that if that should have happened, if I had been greeted by collapsed towers and walls with charred, gaping windows and trees that had been pulled up by their roots, what gradually had become myself would have ceased to exist. Through the years all I stood for, my experience of beauty and of fundamental values, had become crystallized in this wonderful place.

At this point you may naturally ask if I didn't already have anyone to share it with, but since we have agreed to be utterly frank, I am compelled to confide to you that in this respect I was thoroughly lonely. Of course I knew almost everyone worth knowing among the artists and scholars, but such people are unable to share anything with others. Their whole life is spent precisely in not sharing, in not parting with anything without getting something back, in not letting anything near them that can divert them from their way to the top. They could admire my estate, to be sure, and nod appreciatively at my art collection, but the whole time they were appraising it in relation to what they themselves had or could hope to have. So I'm not even sure I wanted to try sharing this precious possession with them.

But what about your family? you will certainly object. Isn't what's precious the very thing you share with those nearest you? Again I'm compelled to be frank, even if it pains me this time, and tell you that especially among my so-called nearest I was perhaps most lonely. In the end I hardly knew my children any more, for they spent most of their time on the Riviera or in the divorce courts, and Lady Euphemia, my wife, I usually met only at receptions where it was correct for us to be seen together, or once in a great while in passing at the estate. Any allusion to an art that wasn't a topic of conversation in her circle at that point of time merely bored her, and nature was for her nothing but a distasteful obstruction one had to breach on the way to or from a dinner or a performance at the opera, where it was important to be seen.

It should be mentioned, Robert Turner continued in a voice which to begin with was almost inaudible, that it hadn't always been like that. I can still remember like a distant dream a time when we could sit together at night and discuss the function of art and make plans for turning the dilapidated estate she had then recently inherited into a focal point for those who fought for man's liberation through music, art and literature. I was so young then that I imagined one could have a world-picture, and I hadn't yet seen that we have pictures only of our own world. I believed that the battlefield of the future was more important than the peace that the masters of the past give us, and in my immaturity I thought, with touching sincerity, that our place was at the barricades and I hadn't understood that actually we can do nothing – can only try to create a lagoon of beauty that finally can become ourselves.

But then you met your Eurydice, said his guest in a low voice.

Robert Turner raised his eyes and looked at him. The way we walked together across the churchyard in the twilight, I should have called her my Beatrice, for although we didn't touch each other, I felt the same appalling nearness as when she laid her hand on me by my grave. She had nothing of the beauty and grace that marked, for instance, the statue of the nude young girl I had had erected in the churchyard, and yet she was like an answer to a longing I had borne unconsciously within me from my earliest youth, as a secret source of my unwritten sonnets, as an inspired subject for my never-created, immortal works of art. The strange thing was that when we came to the grounds of the estate, which I had thought would charm her as if they were fairy-tale woods, she was completely unmoved, and I myself looked at them with new eyes. The trees were only trees, and the lily ponds only lily ponds, not inseparable parts of me. The same thing happened when we approached the house, where lights in some of the top floor windows in the west wing indicated that Lady Euphemia was obviously dressing to go to some late dinner or other.

With its hunting trophies, its old hand-made weapons and a sculpture of a dying stag, the great hall had always been my pride. But my Beatrice stood there in the middle of the floor without casting so much as a glance at any of it. Had it been anyone else but this ignorant child, I should have been astonished, for even the most blasé of Lady Euphemia's so-called friends usually admired, at least secretly, the magnificent antlers and the carving on the gun-stocks. But they were of no consequence to her, and in a strange way the trophies, as well as the weapons and the masterly stag sculpture – by the nineteenth-century artist Antoine-Louis Barye – were changed into something alien. Into something that didn't concern me.

A trifle disturbed by this, I then took her with me into the largest of the rooms and lit the lights, even some candles in a pair of elegant old candelabra on a shelf over the fireplace, to show her my collection of marvellous pictures by Flemish masters – a portrait by Van Dyck for one – and a pair of early works by our own Gainsborough. Also a small painting by El Greco, a gift from a Spanish cabinet minister I had once saved from death in dramatic circumstances and which I naturally valued owning for that reason, but which had never actually appealed to me. The abnormally luminous, contrasting colours and the distorted awkwardness of El Greco's forms wrenched him loose not only from his own time but also from reality, as you will undoubtedly agree. That's probably why some of the so-called artists of the present day derive their notions specifically from this Greek exile, when they have lost their foothold and seek an externally modernistic originality.

Oddly enough it was at this very painting that the child stopped, though she had hardly an inkling who El Greco was. With almost dreamy eyes she looked at the unnaturally long, morbidly ethereal faces, and she gently stretched out her hand and touched one of them, as if trying to relieve the pain that the dark eyes and the half-open mouth were intended to express. For a moment it even seemed she would start crying.

What in God's name is the matter with the child? I thought. But at the same time – and it's still quite incomprehensible to me – I was moved as well. Whether it was because of the child or the painting, I can't tell you, though I think I saw something in the pale faces that I hadn't seen before. Actually, you know, they're rather expressionless, with their lack of naturalistic details, so it must have been something I put into them. One of those modern absurdities, again, about interaction between the work of art and the observer. As if an observer could endow a work with something that's not already there! To regain my senses, I looked at the Van Dyck portrait, which with its cool composure always gave me such peace of mind. But this time I saw only an unknown person staring at me distantly from the wall, and then when I moved my eyes on to the Gainsborough paintings and those by my Flemish masters – whom I had always loved, of course – it was as if they were about to suffocate me with their insistent, aloof indifference.

Suddenly my Beatrice turned towards me, with cheeks that blazed in the light from the candelabra. That slender, but at the same time strong, body trembled as if from cold and yet radiated a moving softness I should have called concern in an adult. Though perhaps a child's the very one who can express it openly even in such moments. What she said was a strangely confirming answer to my despair: It's like a grave!

What do you mean by that? I whispered, even though I realized what she thought – understood what, precisely because of her childlike innocence, she had seen I was surrounded by.

This horrible house, she said and turned towards the El Greco painting. Can't you see how those poor people suffer inside these cold walls? Can't you see the tears I tried to brush away?

My God, I said, painted figures can't cry.

But it's your tears. Don't you understand that?

Of course I should just have smiled at this childish foolishness and naïvety, but to my surprise I felt the tears begin to flow, just as they had that day in the churchyard after she had stroked my cheek. And yet I wasn't so deeply shaken as I had been out there by my grave. It was more as if I had expected it – not the tears exactly, but that strangely naked feeling that all I had loved as part of myself, perhaps even instead of myself, had suddenly become completely alien to me. As if this strange child – she who had been my Beatrice on the way there – had been transformed into an elf and with the touch of a wand had released me from a spell. At the same time I knew of course that it was mad, when I thought what it had cost me to put that old, tumbledown estate into almost regal condition, to transform those overgrown grounds into a marvellous park where poets and scholars sought peace and inspiration, to procure art for which many a museum would have paid a fortune.

And yet I couldn't free myself from a feeling of amazing relief. I'm not, as you have possibly realized, a religious man. But I felt as I imagine the Apostles must have felt when they cast aside everything at Christ's command and followed him! Or perhaps still more as when death has torn one away from the body's heavy shell and one is completely free – something I've experienced, as I remember mentioning to you on our first evening. Consequently I was in a spiritual state that caused me not the slightest alarm, but on the contrary made me feel that it was the only natural thing to do, when I saw this child – like a mind-liberating Joan of Arc – seize one of the candelabra and hold it against the curtains, which instantly caught fire.

I see by your face that you don't believe me, that you don't understand why I didn't tear the candelabrum away from her, and now, afterwards, I must admit that it strikes me too as a mediocre melodrama, a hysterical whim that I should have stopped. But standing there facing my Joan of Arc, I became as if bewitched both by her and by the liberating simplicities of unreality, and so, intoxicated by her resolution, I seized the other candelabrum myself.

It is incredible, Robert Turner continued with a little smile and as calmly as if he were explaining a scientifically interesting phenomenon, how quickly fire spreads, even in a stone building. Of course we went from room to room with the candelabra and set fire to whatever would burn, but it took hardly any time for the old house to be completely enveloped in flames. At last the heat became unbearable, tongues of fire licked up from the floors as one imagines the flames of hell doing, and the roof beams toppled down over us like flaming swords. Not a second too soon, we sprang towards the main entrance, where the heat had already made the hinges bend, so that we barely managed to open the heavy oak door.

Outside, the mild night air seemed like an ice-bath when we stood under the trees on the far side of one of the ponds, where the rain of sparks hissed against the surface of the water. Huge flames lit up the grounds, so they became like a flat stage backdrop with dazzling lights and sharp shadows. The small towers, which had made the house look like a little castle, collapsed, and from the tall windows the fire flew as from the gaping jaws of a fairy-tale dragon.

I stood as if bewitched and watched the annihilation of what I had felt was myself – the heretic's bonfire where my treachery and hypocrisy had been burned. But would a purified me rise like a phoenix from the ashes? Would a clean and naked me have the power to step from the grave as if after an atonement? Would there still be something I could call myself?

Then I saw a figure silhouetted in black against the flaming mass inside a window on the top floor of the west wing. It was Lady Euphemia. Although she was outlined there against the shining background, she was no longer the Lady Euphemia I had met only as a stranger in corridors and at receptions, but the young, moving woman I now knew I had once loved, and who – an eternity ago – I had dreamed with in those overgrown woods and in that tumbledown house. As if petrified, I stared at her, where she stood helplessly swaying, surrounded by flames in the open window, and suddenly there was a scream . . . not a scream raised in terror of death, but as a plea – as if in grief over a life that hadn't been. That I had never given her.

In a wild hope that this slender and unusually tall being, who had just plunged burning to the earth, had taken root in the child – yes, had actually been within her since the day I met her in the churchyard – in that wild hope, I looked around me for my Eurydice, my Beatrice, my Joan of Arc, but I couldn't find her anywhere. Instead, I saw that the entire grounds were full of people who, attracted by the glow in the night sky, had come up from the village to look at the all-consuming fire, and I screamed to them to go away. That this had nothing to do with them!

Then, but without being even the least surprised, as if it too were a confirmation I had been waiting for, I felt a firm grip on my arms, and two uniformed men led me away through the dread-filled crowd.

The lentil soup seemed to taste excellent to Robert Turner. He ate it slowly and with a relish that made it difficult to realize that only a few minutes before he had concluded his agonizing confidence about the fire that had undoubtedly transformed his life. His guest glanced at him from time to time and reflected on how incomprehensible it was that a person could change so utterly in the space of a moment. As if the mere sight of the smoking soup had brushed from his mind the memory of despair and his appalling experience.

Because they had had to wait so long for the soup, the veal with courgettes and noodles was placed on the table the instant they put down their spoons. Therefore there was no opportunity for Robert Turner to ask his guest to offer some new example of his amusing literary work, as he expressed it. But whether he felt it to be any great loss must remain unsaid. As far as the guest was concerned, however, it was a great relief. To tell the truth, he had managed to enjoy the tasty lentils only to a very limited degree, for he had been struggling the whole time to think out something he could tell his host while they sat waiting for the main course. Something that might seem to be a story he had written or on which had been working.

Even after he had returned to the hotel, he couldn't calm down at all, for he knew that the rapid service had given him only a postponement. When they had risen from the table and the guest had politely thanked his host for another exquisite meal, Robert Turner had even said that he looked forward to hearing him tell a new, interesting story on the following evening. . . . But about what?

In the hope of finding something else to occupy his thoughts, he sat down on the little balcony outside his hotel room and remained seated there, looking out over the town. A few lights enabled him to recognize absent-mindedly the quay and the castle and some of the streets he usually walked. He also recognized the silhouette of some tall trees that stood by the pavement close to the table where, only half an hour before, he had sat eating veal, whose taste he had forgotten – or whether he had been at all capable of tasting any of it – and with that his thoughts went back again to Robert Turner, who looked forward to hearing him tell a new and amusing story. Again and again he tried to find something diverting to think about, but Robert Turner's expectant words rose ever more frequently to the surface of his consciousness, and at last he simply gave up.

Then slowly something began to formulate inside him. Actually he had thought about it already while he was struggling with the veal, courgettes and noodles, but it hadn't been with the intention of relating anything. On the contrary, it merely struck him as a contrast with the meal he was busy consuming, and at the same time it had occurred to him, as an almost blasphemous notion, that in spite of the difference there was a curious similarity. The old leftovers from a freezer he had eaten that time had nothing to do with the steaming soup and the delicate meat Robert Turner caused to be conjured up on the table, and the dreary apartment was as far removed as was possible from that exotic street café in a town by the Aegean Sea. The positively starved, indifferent man with whom he had then sat, a kind of friend one might perhaps have called him, had hardly any external points of similarity to that eloquent, aesthetic man of the world, Robert Turner; and yet, after all, there must have been a reason for his happening to think of the man just then, after God knows how many years. . . .

Could there have been something in what Robert Turner had so intimately confided to him about his life and about his life-giving Eurydice that had caused him to remember that lonely, illusionless friend? Perhaps the dark, swaying figure in the window of the burning mansion? Or was it just that his thoughts had been roaming about wildly on the hunt for something he could give the impression of having made up?

No matter the reason, in any case he couldn't possibly tell his host about it, use it as an amusing story between two courses. What would that starved friend have said then? Would he have forgiven him for exhibiting his helpless, naked, life-weary soul as a kind of repayment for a tasty meal? On the other hand he would never of course come to know about it . . . and perhaps one could tamper a bit with reality. Let the apartment be small and humble instead of large and lavish, and let the woman who now and then visited him be young and innocent, not middle aged and manipulative, as he had the impression she had been. Maybe then it would even become truer than reality or, rather, throw reality into relief, for in a way it would give depth to what had made such a strong impression on him at the time and had caused him to think he should have gone to see the man again. Which he had never dared to do.

The thought of all this filled him with so strange an unease that he almost felt he *was* Joseph Frost – that he had the power to cause reality to become still more real – and when, after having gone to bed, he lay there all keyed up and tried to sleep, he remembered more and more about the dinner with the man who might perhaps be called a friend. At last he could picture quite clearly how he had looked – much older than himself, despite the fact that they were of the same age, and with a thin and wrinkled neck that stuck out of a not entirely clean shirt. He could also hear quite distinctly, as if the man sat in a corner of the half-dark room, that faint voice which spoke with apparent indifference about a life that had turned into a grave, out of which he hadn't the strength to climb. Into an existence that had lost all meaning. . . . But hadn't Robert Turner also spoken about such a grave?

Forgive me, he said to the form there in the darkness, but I think I'll have to tell your story in spite of everything, for even if he couldn't be more different from you, the man who'll hear it tomorrow evening may be able to see . . . may understand. . . .

He searched for the right words, for what would give the story a meaning. But before he found the words, if indeed he ever would have done so, he fell into a deep sleep and lay there as though unconscious until the next morning.

THE FOURTH
EVENING

▣　▣　▣　▣

THE emaciated man who, the evening before, had almost felt he was Joseph Frost, didn't wake up until the day was far advanced and the sun shone in upon him. The instant he opened his eyes he remembered Robert Turner's friendly words about looking forward to hearing him tell a new, interesting story and, relieved, he thought of the solution he had found just before he went to sleep. But when he tried to remember what he had actually thought while he was lying there in the darkness, it became more and more vague and remote to him. It was like a jigsaw puzzle one has been quite certain how to put together and for which suddenly one can no longer find the right pieces. What in the evening had seemed so clear was now just totally chaotic. True enough he faintly remembered that, out of respect for the man who might once have been a friend, he had thought he should try to describe differently the woman who came and went. Maybe the friend's apartment too. But would it be enough merely to change her age? Or to let the apartment be small and cramped instead of large and desolate? And would such an alteration of reality actually add anything at all to the narrative, as he had imagined in his state of elation? Even the fact that he had thought of the story because there had been a remarkable similarity between his friend and Robert Turner seemed completely meaningless now in the full light of day – for what, one wonders, could a self-deceiver who was unfit for life have to do with a man who enjoyed life like the utterly frank professor?

His whole day was spent in trying to find his way back to what had been so obvious to him the previous evening. Above all, he tried to remember what he had been thinking about immediately before he had fallen asleep – that business about its being something Robert Turner would certainly understand. But he got no further than he had actually done just as he fell asleep, to words he somehow had on his tongue but couldn't speak . . . and maybe it had simply been something like a dream. And yet he couldn't escape the thought that he had seen something, had noticed something in his host's eyes and way of expressing himself, when he had told him about the fire and talked about his Eurydice, that couldn't be imagination. He couldn't escape the thought that there *had* been something he had seen that maybe Robert Turner himself didn't even see or in any case tried to conceal. And he had the almost intoxicating feeling that he was on the verge of becoming the Joseph Frost that he in a thoughtless moment and without understanding why had said he was.

But no matter how much he struggled to catch sight again of what he thought he had seen, he found no foothold for the leap into Joseph Frost's world. Gradually as the hours passed he became in reality more and more his actual self: a man who had never written a line, except for some letters and a couple of descriptions in connection with his work, and he became still more despondent than he had been when he woke up. It was as if the thoughts and suspicions he had had in the darkness the previous evening, instead of bringing him closer to his goal, which till then hadn't been a goal at all, made that goal both clear and unattainable for him because of the hopelessness he felt when he awakened.

Nevertheless, when it finally began to grow dark and the time approached for his dinner with Robert Turner, he left the hotel and walked down towards the harbour. But as he approached the restaurant, his steps gradually became slower and slower, and when he came to the square with Hippocrates' tree, he stopped and sat down on the low wall beneath it. For what should he do? What should he say when his host leaned back after ordering the first course and asked him to tell a new, interesting story?

He was unaware how long he sat like that without finding any way out except simply turning back to the hotel and forgetting about dinner. Now and then his thoughts drifted, so that he almost sat there sleeping, or else he looked helplessly at the old buildings that surrounded the square. One of them looked like a church, but it was obviously a mixture of police station and town hall, for uniformed officers came and went continually, and outside men in dark suits sat at several small tables and argued excitedly until one or other of them looked at the clock, seized a brief-case and walked quickly into the building, as if going to a meeting. He noticed that some of the men were drinking coffee, which was served by an old man with a purse on his belt, and he rose hesitantly to go over and ask if he could buy a cup too.

Then he saw Robert Turner. He was standing with his back half turned to him and looking at Hippocrates' tree as if it were a work of art, tilting his head as if to get a better view of it behind all the supports that surrounded that fragile tree like bars. Then he said in a voice that seemed to suggest he had been aware all the time of the emaciated man with whom he would soon be dining and was merely continuing an amusing conversation: If I must give an honest opinion, I'm inclined to believe that our friend Hippocrates never sat under this tree, but the legend about his doing so seems undeniably moving. Don't you agree? It's almost as if he's still sitting there and I've paid him a visit to be cured of some painful illness. And you can be sure he would have had a remedy for this Courths-Mahler's Disease of yours too.

Robert Turner cast an amiably questioning glance at his guest, who realized that his cheeks were becoming hot and thought that, with any luck, his host believed he was blushing because of his illness. But it was because he felt himself caught trying to sneak away from the dinner and the expectation of a new and interesting story, and he felt that was really what was behind Robert Turner's apparently amiable remarks. For a moment he considered saying that, unfortunately, he couldn't dine with him that evening, that he had another appointment. But what kind of appointment could it be? Robert Turner knew, of course, that he was not acquainted with anyone but him in this little town. So, uneasy in his mind, he followed the slightly older man down towards the harbour.

When they had sat down at their usual table at the restaurant and the young waiter had come with cutlery and water and shown them a menu, Robert Turner said with studied graciousness: This evening I think it should be your turn to decide what we shall eat. How thoughtless of me not to have suggested it before.

The guest managed only to shake his head.

But my dear Frost, said Robert Turner and handed him the menu, don't be so modest now! True enough, I have greater experience than you, perhaps, where Greek food is concerned, but a man with your imagination and powers of observation has no doubt taken note of this country's distinctive qualities even in the culinary field – if for no other reason, then at least for the sake of your writing. What do you suggest?

The guest understood that this was not to be avoided either, and because he felt that Robert Turner was making fun of him, or perhaps even embarrassing him intentionally to intimate that he saw through him, he became still more desperate than he already was because he knew he would be forced to tell a story. He took the menu and looked over it in confusion. He couldn't make head or tail of it; what he might possibly have understood vanished as if in a fog because of Robert Turner's graciously expectant gaze. It was as when a father watches his child sit down at the piano and in blind pride waits to hear a new Mozart reveal himself. Nevertheless, he finally managed to read the name of one of the dishes and mumbled haltingly: *Kotopoulo yemisto.*

Robert Turner beamed. Splendid! he exclaimed. You couldn't possibly have made a choice that would have pleased me more. Stuffed capon is one of my favourite dishes. Perhaps it sounds strange but I think it gives me a special pleasure to know that we are dining on a castrated cock which has never had that obtrusive cockiness cocks usually have. Besides, the time it takes to prepare and stuff it with pine kernels, raisins, sliced onion and minced liver will give us ample opportunity to hear one of those interesting stories of yours. But to start with we must naturally have a first course, no matter how small, so what would you fancy suggesting?

You must choose that, the guest said quickly.

No, no! This is *your* dinner, after all, and I'm certain that you already have something in mind that can sharpen our appetite for the fat capon.

A light soup was the hesitant reply.

Splendid, beamed Robert Turner. But what kind?

The guest cast an uneasy, almost imploring eye up at the head waiter who had approached the table and was standing ready with pad and pencil, but he received no intimation of help. Then he tried again to study the menu, but even if it was written in English as well as Greek, it was as if he had never seen the words before. After a while he heard the head waiter clear his throat and said in a whisper what he had at that very moment managed to spell out for himself in Greek: *Avgolemono psarosoupa.*

Interesting, said Robert Turner and moved his lips as if he were tasting it in his thoughts. Undoubtedly interesting, even if I wouldn't call it a light soup because of the eggs. But the fish and especially the lemon decidedly bear witness to an artist's flair for contrasts – not least if one can in fact have the capon stuffed with liver.

Again the guest felt he was being made fun of, but the thought that perhaps it took a long time to cook the soup and that he would therefore have to try to tell a story even before they received it made him forget the hidden irony he suspected behind Robert Turner's apparently laudatory remark about the artist's flair for contrasts. When he noticed Robert Turner leaning forward to pour the wine – which he, fortunately, hadn't been asked to order – his chest tightened.

Robert Turner raised his glass and said: A toast to the story-teller Joseph Frost!

The guest closed his eyes while he drank, not to be able to taste the wine better, for he couldn't taste anything, but to try to remember what he had thought just as he fell asleep the night before. But that was quite impossible and, almost as if in a trance, he merely began to tell a story.

Mogens Klint almost never saw anyone except in his home or at his place of employment, for he had few or no friends. Still more rarely did anyone happen to ring him up and ask him for something – a favour, for instance, or a piece of advice. But one day a person Mogens Klint thought he might call a friend actually rang him. What they talked about to begin with he was not in a position to remember later, for all that had been supplanted by the last thing the friend said before he hung up: But listen, before we ring off. There was something I sat brooding about at breakfast the other day, and I thought I must discuss that with Mogens! Just can't think what it was, but it must have been something important, I suppose! Long pause. Then he suddenly exclaimed: Yes, now I remember what it was. It was Life! It was simply Life it struck me I ought to talk to you about. That all right with you, some evening next week?

Then Mogens Klint heard himself say: Maybe I could come over for dinner? But he said it not without a certain blushing uneasiness, for he was worried that the proposal might be taken as an intrusive attempt to restore something that had probably been a friendship. Besides, he became bewildered merely at the thought of what in the world he would manage to say about Life.

When, some days later, they sat down at the table in the little bachelor apartment, Mogens Klint noticed that his friend looked considerably older than when he had last seen him. Whenever that was. A thin and wrinkled neck projected from a not quite clean shirt. Grey, unkempt hair. Eyes quite without focus. His friend smiled to himself, as if he happened to think of something he couldn't quite remember. Good you invited yourself to dinner, he said. Gives Life a kind of meaning somehow, to offer food to old friends. Had almost forgotten you existed, as a matter of fact.

And I thought you had killed yourself.

As if he remembered what had made him smile: Certainly stood at the window and thought about it the other day – whether I should jump out. Felt it was too disgusting. Squashed against the pavement, spread all over. Blood, brains, the lot. Who would bother to scrape a chap up? I could have been lying there for years. What's more, my psychiatrist thinks it would have been a lousy solution. Bad for his reputation, I take it. Worried about unemployment. It's really quite a laugh. For years a chap thinks seriously about killing himself – maybe he's so alive it hurts to live. Then one day he loses interest in it. In killing himself, I mean. A chap's got enough to do with getting up in the morning, with imagining he's working, with ruining his liver at moderate expense. Whisky has got so damned expensive, and as time goes on, that worries a chap more than how he will put an end to it. . . . To Life, that is. . . . Hope the food tastes good anyway. It was something I had in the freezer, which I want to empty. Stupid to lie here with a full freezer if I bring it off, after all.

But lord, you have your books, don't you, and your gramophone records?

He tasted the mixed vegetables cautiously, uncertain whether it was worth bothering to eat them. At last he apparently decided not to touch them.

My books? Sometimes I try to read them, but they get less and less interesting. They try to describe Life, and what good is that to me? Why should I need to read page after page about something I've got quite enough of – loneliness, human debasement, sex without love and too much liquor. All of it mixed up together like these vegetables, only with different packaging, taken right out of the various so-called writers' freezers of people's lives. If only there had been a little elegance and refinement. But no, the whole thing is served flat on a dish.

Speaking of refinement, said Mogens Klint with a feeling of boldness, as if he were moving into a world he didn't know at all, is it true you've got yourself a girl-friend? A young person barely twenty, if one trusts the rumours flying around?

His friend looked out of the window.

That must have been some years ago. Or last week. Or maybe yesterday? It's hard to remember everything. Besides, she's so damned young, you know – has smooth skin, of course, and long blonde hair. Fairly inexperienced, for that matter. But she expects me to do something Meaningful. Take a doctor's degree, write a book, compose a piano concerto, travel to Africa. The last is her favourite idea. We could go to Tanzania, she says, and you could teach physics at the university in Dar es Salaam. Good God, do they have one in a God-forsaken place like that? Anyway, what would they do with physics? And I, she goes on, and I could help fight infant mortality. . . . As if people shouldn't have the chance to die as children, so they can escape living a whole life first! That's the sort of thing she's just too young to understand, so I don't quite know why I let her come.

Mogens Klint asked hesitantly: But don't you sleep with her?

He got up, walked over to the kitchen counter. Then he emptied his untouched food into the refuse bag, rinsed his plate under the tap and put it into the cupboard over the dresser before he replied.

Think so. Not unreasonable, anyway, that that's what's happened, when I wake up well into morning and find the bed-clothes in one big heap at the foot of the bed. But I haven't got as far as asking. For now, I've enough on my hands with this talk about Africa.

Why don't you go? You're tired of teaching the students here – students who always arrive late and drink coffee during lectures as well. Down there you would meet a completely different type. It might be a challenge.

Oh God, not you too! If you've got to moralize, you'd better leave me one of your Doomsday books – which, after all, a chap can put down. Besides, I live here in an apartment that needn't concern me – whose appearance I can hardly remember the second I've gone through the door because it's so gloriously charmless and insignificant. Can't bear to wash it either. Maybe that's why I let her come, because she always says: Now we must get your place washed! Then she does it. Mmm, hadn't thought of that before. Nice to have found a reason for letting her in.

Has she a name, this poor young girl?

Assume so, but to be honest I don't remember it. Call her something new each time. Rosalind or Dido or Carmen. She thinks, God help me, it's a game. Wonder what she'd say if I told her I haven't a clue what she's called. Whether she has any name at all. It's not so good to know about people like that, who just come and go in your life.

He went over to the cabinet with the record-player and radio and came back with a bottle and glass, filled the latter and drank most of its contents with a little grimace.

You probably drive a car, he said, although he knew that Mogens Klint didn't have one, so I'm sure you won't mind me drinking my whisky alone. By the way, she talks about that too – about cirrhosis of the liver and nerve-cells that die by the thousand after every gulp. Why the devil can't they be allowed to? . . . So I hide the bottle behind those antiquated gramophone records over there, or else in the attic or down in the basement. What in God's name made me buy those records? Though once I must have enjoyed it, I suppose. Listening to music, I mean. But last year – or maybe it was a month ago – when I put on a record, it just seemed like a joke. A series of mechanical vibrations that somehow give a kind of emotional experience. I took it off after a few minutes.

He emptied his glass and poured another drink. That's a game, too, he said. My game. Hiding the whisky – now here, now there. Do it every damned day, so a chap can really believe that one day she'll come back.

He emptied his glass again. But now I suppose you ought to be going soon, anyway. Far as I remember, you've got a wife and a couple of teenage kids that possibly miss you. A chap can never tell, can he? Besides, I've got something or other to do, I think . . . whatever it is. You'll see it has something to do with the window. After all, it's not inconceivable that one day I'll have enough Life in me to use it.

No one will ever know if that was supposed to be the end of the story. Even the guest was uncertain, all along, about how it would continue and was almost astounded that words and sentences came almost without his thinking of them. There were moments when he felt more like a listener than a story-teller, so strange was it to feel an almost forgotten memory come to life in his own mouth. When he had got as far as the friend's uncertain words about perhaps having enough Life in him one day to use the window, he paused to try to remember if he himself had said or done anything to give his friend's life substance. For that's what one needs, after all. But he couldn't remember saying or doing anything, and yet perhaps he should have made a kind of ending, for it was no longer just something he had once experienced, but a story he was telling to another person. Perhaps that person needed him to have done something? Needed to hear that it wasn't just a matter of standing around waiting for enough Life to let you jump out of the window? But what should he put into the story, when he couldn't remember having done anything at all, and didn't even know what he should have done?

It was precisely because the guest paused there and sat thinking about how he should give his story a meaningful ending that Robert Turner seized the opportunity and made a discreet sign to the head waiter. The thought of the steaming fish soup had gradually made him rather preoccupied, and actually it became more and more unimportant to him what was going to happen to this man who didn't even know the names of the people with whom he spent the night. In fact, it occurred to him that his guest ought to let him jump out of the window as soon as possible, so the soup could be brought to the table!

Finally it was indeed, and Robert Turner let the head waiter give him a generous helping before directing him on to his guest. But the guest wouldn't have any soup. Not even the head waiter's slightly raised eyebrows induced him to take so much as a ladleful, for he was thinking only of what he should have said to his friend, or at least should have said he had said. He became especially preoccupied when it struck him that, after that dinner, he hadn't heard a word from the man and that he had done nothing either to find out how things had gone with him. To find out whether he simply existed any more. Could one have been someone's friend if one didn't try to find that out?

The question gave him a feeling of shame that made him ill, and this illness was probably the reason that, for the first time in the course of those evenings, he felt an aversion to his host. Robert Turner had earnestly asked him to tell a story, and during a pause – which possibly had been a bit long – he had at once given the impression of thinking the story was over, and now he sat eating fish soup as if he had never heard about that poor man's meaningless, despairing life. He didn't even allow himself to notice that the guest couldn't eat any of the soup, but enjoyed every last spoonful himself, as if it were the object of existence.

When Robert Turner at last laid down his spoon, wiped his mouth lightly with his napkin and said that it was one of the best soups he had eaten in a long time, his guest responded only with an almost imperceptible nod. He felt no desire to talk and just hoped that the stuffed capon would be served, so that the meal could be over and done with as quickly as possible. But Robert Turner completely disregarded the guest's withdrawn attitude; he was in an apparently excellent humour and made amiable remarks to the young waiter who cleared the table. When the waiter had gone, he filled both glasses, even that of his guest, who had hardly touched his wine, leaned well back in his chair and gave the impression that he thought the time had now come to contribute his part of the evening's conversation.

The story you told, began Robert Turner, about this man who didn't dare take his life, was obviously a kind of short story you are preoccupied with. Literature certainly isn't my line, but it's possible I have a modest notion of the function of art, and so I shall venture to give you a bit of advice. First, however, I shall admit that as a matter of fact I have faith in you, for you don't try to make your readers uneasy with world problems they can't solve in the slightest, but write only about the loneliness and longings that are the intellectuals' more elegant variants of common literature's sentimental dreams. You have no tiresome political bias either, and you are good enough to seem interesting, but nevertheless aren't threatening. One knows, in short, where one is with you, and so you will undoubtedly go far as a writer.

But with regard to the story you have just sketched, I should indeed recommend a thorough revision before you let it out of your hands. It had, perhaps, a sort of trendy atmosphere, but it was difficult for me to find in it anything but an attempt to tramp along the tedious, sociorealistic paths that the guilt-ridden writers of our day have turned into a kind of highway of atonement. Why, it described the central character as a piece of flotsam without will, dignity or spirit, a being entirely in the hands of circumstances. You must excuse me but I didn't find a word of it that could open the reader's mind to the worthy, exalted action suicide can in reality be.

But he was like that, the guest said sullenly.

Robert Turner raised his eyebrows. Oh lord! Naturally I also realize that individuals may kill themselves because they are dragging out their life on a rubbish-heap like the chap you depicted in this poetic attempt of yours. But why should that interest us?

Because it's true, mumbled the guest restlessly.

True! said Robert Turner. But haven't you learned as an artist that truth must be used for something meaningful? ... Look, for example, at the etchings and woodcuts of this Kathe Kollwitz, who continually depicts the starved and filthy children of the proletariat. *She*'s dead, of course, but those emaciated begging children, you know, stare at people from the walls of virtually every museum and, I ask you, for what purpose? You can see children like that anywhere in the world.

We need no Kathe Kollwitz to remind us of their existence. What we need, on the contrary, is an art that can give us a feeling of man's greatness, so that a person – if he really wants to – can gain strength to fight against the distress of which these children are supposed to be some kind of evidence – an art that might also get children like that to *do* something instead of just standing around staring at us. But it's as if the artists in our day don't want to see man's greatness, as if they aren't able to see the individualists for fear of failing the masses. And yet the individualists are Light dwelling amongst us!

The individualist I shall now tell you about as a kind of illuminating contrast to the leading character in your attempt at a short story is, I admit, dead, but precisely by choosing death he showed us mankind's life-giving greatness. As you've perhaps already grasped, even if you've possibly had little contact with English theatre, I'm thinking of Sir Edmund Radcliffe, who died by his own hand after a radiant première of *King Lear*, in which he played the title role. The incident was naturally discussed in all the newspapers of the world, and the most improbable speculations about the cause of this tragic conclusion to a sensational career were advanced, but the truth never came out. Only one person knew it – namely, myself.

Those last words came in an undertone, as if it troubled him to speak them, and as if to divert attention from himself still more, he bent forward over the table and poured more wine for his guest.

Did he really take his own life?

Robert Turner ignored his guest's question. Then he raised his glass and drank carefully, and as he sat there afterwards studying the small bubbles in the lightly effervescing local wine, he continued the story: Sir Edmund was a quite exceptional actor who knew his profession better than anyone I know. One often says that great actors *are* their roles – that they grow into them with their whole being. But that's only from the viewpoint of the ignorant. The really gifted actor *isn't* his roles – he shapes them on the basis of his experience, his knowledge and his cool control of himself as an instrument. Young people, for whom the stage is still only like a springboard to fame, or old drudges who have stumbled in their own spring through lack of talent, can gush out that they are made for such and such a part because they themselves have experienced some of what they seem to find in the character they want to play, or because they think they can *feel* the character's nature from within themselves. Even in that first outburst – that they are made for the part – they have revealed their lack of professional insight. No one is made for a part – he must make it himself. No actor can *be* a character on the stage any more than a sculptor can be his statue or a writer his novel, for he must stand the same distance from what he depicts as the painter does from his canvas and the writer from his words. He must *use* his feelings and his experiences, not be used by them – the way a man is who doesn't know his profession – and he must be conscious of how he uses them.

The guest bent cautiously forward and opened his mouth to say something. He couldn't follow this long explanation of the actor's art, as his head was filled the whole time with the thought of the man who had killed himself backstage.

Robert Turner, however, appeared not to notice his attempt to speak. It was this realization, he continued, that made Sir Edmund an individualist in his field, and therefore he could play almost anything. But the moment he had left the theatre, he was always completely himself. One never saw him performing as if he were on-stage, the way some actors are fond of doing in daily life. If he played Falstaff, for example, he didn't noisily wolf down tablefuls of food at parties, and when he played Hamlet – which he did countless times of course – he didn't dress up in black tights and go walking up and down the street with wrinkled brow and solemn tread while reading self-importantly from a book. But of course that doesn't mean he was unaffected by his roles. On the contrary, he worked on them day and night, immersed himself in their aesthetic possibilities, made himself familiar with even the most trivial details to gain an accurate image of the times and read other works by the author of the piece besides, in order to understand the part better by those means. If he was to portray an historical figure, he always paid me a visit, asking me to show him paintings and other art from that person's period, so that the shaping of the character could be as perfect as possible. Very often he spent night after night with me out at the house which, as I mentioned, unfortunately burned down. We discussed the play out there and all the parts – right up to sunrise. His goal was absolute perfection, and in principle he approached each new part as if it were his first, so that routine wouldn't make rehearsals light and superficial. Not infrequently the two of us were amused at people's ingratiating questions about how he managed to create such perfect characters – about whether it was a rare, innate gift or the result of superhuman powers of insight. Then he always answered with a little smile, which was so characteristic of him, that he had a little trick – Work!

But then how could he kill himself when he had achieved so much? the guest ventured.

But Robert Turner ignored him once again.

Strangely enough, he had never played King Lear before, although he knew that from his tenderest youth he had wanted to with his whole heart, and even if his modesty naturally forbade him to think like that, he should have realized that it was in that very role two geniuses would meet – Sir Edmund and William Shakespeare. A hint of such a meeting must nevertheless have been in his mind, for never had I seen him so nervous – so keyed up and incredibly energetic – during the preparation of a role. It was as if he spared no effort to make the poet's intentions and his own interpretation produce a higher, inspired unity – a fusion no one had ever experienced. Even perfection was no longer enough! Hour after hour he scrutinized paintings and drawings from the twelfth, thirteenth and fourteenth centuries – the play is based on an old Celtic legend, you know – so he could work out an absolutely correct costume, and he insisted that the King's magnificent jewellery should be genuine, not lack-lustre imitations. No one at the theatre escaped his advice and demands, and if they all hadn't had such great respect for him and valued his insight as well, such wholesale meddling would hardly have been tolerated.

As for myself, said Robert Turner, after taking another sip of wine from the glass that he still held in his hand,

I have always liked *A Midsummer Night's Dream* best of all Shakespeare's plays, for in beauty, charm and subtlety it surpasses everything else he wrote. It was written, after all – as you undoubtedly remember – before the poet's mind was darkened by a deplorable pessimism. But I must admit that *King Lear* can form the basis of a production that is even more impressive. . . . Just think of the possibilities in the designing of Lear's castle as a setting for kings and princesses, dukes and earls, all dressed in the most sumptuous costumes, and in the devising of heaths and woods which, in their bewitching wildness, naturally make a more overwhelming and picturesque impression than the charming woodlands that frame the innocent love and frolic of *A Midsummer Night's Dream.*

Robert Turner stopped and sat looking dreamily in front of him, as if the lamps on the restaurant tables and along the quay were footlights, and the old Crusaders' fortress were Lear's or Gloucester's castle. The guest followed his glance in the vague hope of seeing something that might make it easier for him to understand what his host was talking about, but he saw nothing except the fishing- and pleasure-boats, and the ruin of the fortress. In the course of Robert Turner's narrative it had slowly dawned on him that, once in his youth, he must have been at the theatre and seen this play, but the only thing he remembered was a blind man staggering through a wood and something about some daughters who had betrayed him.

This King Lear, asked the guest, was he blind?

Robert Turner turned slowly towards him. No, he answered coolly. As you will certainly remember on closer reflection, it was the Earl of Gloucester who was blinded, and by one of fate's strange coincidences his evil and illegitimate son was also called Edmund – something that made a few journalists advance the completely ludicrous theory that Sir Edmund must have committed suicide because through his encounter with this spineless character, he had recognized the wickedness in his own mind. . . . As if Sir Edmund would have had a single wicked thought in his whole life!

Did he hang himself? asked the guest.

Robert Turner closed his eyes, as though the memory of the gifted actor's death filled him with an unendurable pain. All the muscles in his body tensed, as if to gain control over his feelings, and the guest – frightened – thought he would crush the glass in his hand. But it lasted for only a few seconds; after which he opened his eyes and was himself again, even if his gaze was somewhat preoccupied.

Sir Edmund didn't hang himself, he said calmly. He shot himself before the mirror in his dressing-room, and it was I who found him. As I mentioned, it happened after the première of *King Lear*, and you must try to visualize the situation backstage after the final curtain. The performance was more dazzling than anyone could have imagined, and Sir Edmund's acting as the poor King, especially, surpassed all expectations. He conducted himself more regally than any real king. When he raised his hands in despair, the jewel-studded rings he wore flashed, and when he entered at the end carrying his daughter's body in his arms, the artificial moonlight made the ermine trimming on the hood of his cape shine like a halo around that noble face. From the manager's box, where I always sat when Sir Edmund performed, I could observe both him and the audience, whom I had never indeed seen so thoroughly spellbound by him. No wonder the applause almost didn't stop!

As was to be expected, practically everyone wanted to congratulate him, and the crush backstage was so great that the poor stage-hands just had to delay clearing up after the performance. From the box I had of course easier access to the dressing-rooms than one has from the auditorium, but I preferred to let the young, less well-known admirers go ahead, for their enthusiasm more than mine was the very thing that would convince him how extraordinary his performance had been. When I thought they had taken up enough of his time and walked down to see him, I discovered that they were just standing tightly packed in the corridor outside his dressing-room. The door was locked from the inside! The confusion was considerable, for it was quite unlike Sir Edmund to turn away his public, and no one knew what should be done. Some actor or other – I no longer remember who – had been knocking discreetly for a long time without receiving any kind of answer, and when I came he looked helplessly at me, as if I might offer some explanation.

It might be thought, of course, that after attaining what one could call the high point of his life, Sir Edmund was quite simply unable to see people. That he, if I may put it like this, had been quite shaken by his boundary-shattering artistic performance and therefore felt compelled to remain completely alone. Nevertheless, I couldn't understand why he hadn't shown any signs of life – why he had given no kind of apology or explanation of why he had to remain alone – and an icy dread gripped my chest. Because I had known Sir Edmund practically all my adult life – from long before he was knighted – I was aware of a concealed entrance to his dressing-room that no one else knew about any longer, and – unobserved – I withdrew from the crowd and went in to him through that secret entrance.

The sight that confronted me can be described only with difficulty, and I shall never be able to forget it either. That powerful form – even more impressive dead than alive – lay slumped over the make-up table, and in his hand he held a pistol of the sort used in seventeenth-century plays. He had removed none of his make-up, and the cape with the ermine-trimmed hood still lay over his shoulders. Either he had shot himself when he first came in, while the applause still filled the entire theatre, or he had sat there for a while in front of the mirror with that handsome old pistol aimed at his temple. His face, which lay half turned towards me, had a strange expression, as if it had filled him with endless pain to have to desert both his profession and his mission in life – to act as beauty's link with man. Not only the yellow journalists but some of his so-called friends naturally made out that his facial expression told of a hopelessness and grief like that which King Lear apparently feels because of man's wickedness and a world that is falling apart. In other words, that his sensitivity to the part must have made him see that our times are like that too, and that this awareness was so intense he simply couldn't bear it.

The guest, who had sat motionless the whole time, was uneasy about interrupting his host, not only because it could destroy the experience of the story but because he feared it would be taken as criticism of this man of insight and learning. Besides, he well remembered Robert Turner's disgust the evening before when he told him about the student who had interrupted him in the middle of a lecture. Nevertheless, he asked softly: But is that so unthinkable?

Robert Turner smiled. That is, his mouth might suggest that he did, but his eyes were cold and narrow as he leaned back in his chair. It pains me to have to say it, he said, but now and then you make me doubt that you are a writer, or at any rate that you have any insight into what is supposed to be your field. Obviously I quite understand *King Lear*'s dramatic contents, that the various characters betray each other, that, for instance, the Earl of Gloucester gets his eyes plucked out and even trampled on – something I find unduly repulsive, as a matter of fact – and that when Lear realizes at last that he has rejected and driven to death the only one of his daughters he could rely on, the poor King despairs over the foundering of the world in wickedness and lust for power. This so-called plot, my dear Frost, is however only a skeleton on which the poet spins his imagination's flesh and blood. No one – not even the denim-clad Doomsday prophets of our time – would be able to sit two minutes and listen to such a dirge, if it weren't for Shakespeare's miraculously rich, poetic language. Nor would we have had the patience to sit there, if the poet, by letting his characters interact, had been unable to create a seductive and enriching medieval world of make-believe, where kings and princesses, dukes and earls, magnificent costumes and the elegant art of fencing were the very stuff that bewitched both the child and the connoisseur in us. To entertain and enrich – that's what Shakespeare wanted to achieve, and he achieves it today too.

But, ventured the guest, you spoke, after all, about this King Lear's despair over the foundering of the world. He entered, you said, with his daughter's body in his arms and realized too late that he had rejected and driven to death the very one he should have relied on! Well, couldn't that have made your friend think of whoever it was *he* had rejected?

Robert Turner bent forward over the table. Good God, he said, the world has always foundered, over and over, as long as it has been inhabited by men. And we reject someone every single day. What's the use of constantly telling ourselves that? We know it and we have always known it. . . . Look at the paintings of the crucified Christ. Do you think that for nearly two thousand years artists have been painting this half-naked man nailed to a cross to tell us he was crucified? Of course some people may have imagined that it's necessary to remind ourselves incessantly of this man's sufferings, but the real artists have seen them as a point of departure for the experience they give us of the bold play of lines and the moving richness of colours. After all, the person who looks at these paintings will seldom be gripped by the suffering, but by a moving beauty that is the essence of art.

To his own surprise, the guest didn't give in. Had he rejected someone? he asked.

Robert Turner shrugged. Of course, he said, some people did indeed make a big thing of the fact that Sir Edmund had a daughter people thought he had turned away. Nothing, however, could have been more mistaken than to think he had done so. For obviously he loved her, but with his enormous work-load and need for concentration, it was simply impossible for him to have anyone in the house who constantly implicated him in the distress in Africa, the wars in Central America, the unrest in Northern Ireland and whatever else it is that young people are always talking about today. So he wasn't able to see her. It was as simple as that.

But what happened to her?

I haven't a clue, said Robert Turner. Sir Edmund never spoke of her. But she turned up at the funeral, and then she looked as if she had just got out of bed and pulled on some rags lying on the floor. Moreover, she had some kind of hysterical breakdown and screamed so much that people could scarcely hear a word of the beautiful sonnets I had asked my good friend Dame Eleanor Bird to read by the coffin. All in all she behaved most improperly and did her best to make our final leave-taking of this unique man less poetic and dignified than I had planned.

Why did she cry so much? asked the guest.

I haven't the foggiest idea, said Robert Turner, but some people lose their self-control in situations like that, you know. Needless to say, the journalists went for her when she left the church, and the next day there were large pictures of her in the newspapers under headlines like I HAVE FORGIVEN HIM! and THE SHOT THAT RECONCILED FATHER AND DAUGHTER. It was a notion as egocentrically disgusting as only a young girl of that sort can think up. . . . What in the world did she have to forgive? What kind of reconciliation could be involved?

Robert Turner raised his glass again and drank, this time with a rapid, slightly irritated movement, at the same time as he cast a glance towards the door of the restaurant, as if to see if the stuffed, castrated cock wasn't about to arrive. His face had an impassive, unsympathetic expression, possibly suggesting he actually regretted beginning this story. His guest became uneasy and felt almost guilty of having caused him to do so. Nevertheless, he asked: But why did he take his life? You said that you were the only one who knew that.

That, said Robert Turner, well, frankly, I had expected you as an artist to have understood that without my having to explain it to you. As you may remember, I mentioned that Sir Edmund was an outstanding craftsman. That only perfection was good enough for him. During the *Lear* rehearsals he clearly felt that even perfection would be inadequate. Then what hardly an artist in a thousand experiences even once in a lifetime happened at the première, and he managed what he thought was impossible – he surpassed even perfection! He realized that not only the audience but his fellow-actors were as if spellbound by his acting and that all the people on the stage as well as the auditorium melted together into a higher, inspired unity, thanks to him. At the same time he knew that this was something he would never be equal to again – that everything he did in the future would stand in the shadow of this superhuman achievement. In other words, it wasn't just a triumph, even if it might seem so at the moment, for the demand of others – and not less of himself – for this feat to be repeated would make him feel that all future character building was a stinging defeat, compared with the Lear of this première. That, my dear Frost, was the real tragedy!

His guest almost whispered: Did *he* say that, while he sat in front of the mirror?

No, not that, said Robert Turner.

As these words were spoken they gazed at each other – the story-teller and the listener, the host and his guest – and it was as if no one else existed under the evening sky above this harbour in the Aegean except these two late-middle-aged men. How long they sat like that neither of them would ever be able to say, but it was actually perhaps no more than a few seconds.

At last the guest lowered his eyes. So you were with him when it happened? he said.

Robert Turner didn't answer. If the guest had ventured to look up, he would have noticed that his host's face turned pale, and that his body seemed rigid, except for his lips which trembled slightly. But this, too, lasted for a shorter time than he would have believed if he had not witnessed it.

It's difficult to explain what Sir Edmund meant to me over the years, Robert Turner said in a tone more tense than hitherto his guest had heard him use, but he was – to put it simply – the one person who more than any other kept alive in me my faith in art's true function – to ennoble and exalt. I've already described how his inspired interpretation of King Lear affected me. Well, in just that way he was for me the very incarnation of an art which, by lifting us above the everyday, gives us a perspective on existence that turns the moment's need, catastrophe and suffering merely into unimportant trivia. It's like hovering high in the air like an eagle and looking down on the people of the earth as if they were small, almost invisible insects that kill and breed, that creep and crawl, far below you. But it's not only space that grows bigger – time changes too. The days turn to minutes, the years to hours, the centuries to months, so that all existence gains another dimension, torn free from the life of the individual man – this little flicker in the universe. Your consciousness becomes like a thousand-year-old tree that has seen people be born and die, seen warriors and plagues lay waste about them, but that stands there nevertheless like a steadfast hope, with its roots sunk deep in the earth's origins and its crown raised upward towards the everlasting stars.

When I entered through the secret door, Robert Turner continued, to be the first to congratulate him, he was sitting motionless and looking at himself in the mirror as if he were paralysed. It was as if he were observing a stranger, a person he wanted to have nothing to do with. I couldn't understand why he sat like that, for after all he must have heard the endless cheering and applause.

Edmund, I said, you have never been more radiant.

Never such a traitor either, he whispered.

But for God's sake, you brought the house down!

Yes, he said, still in a low voice and without taking his eyes from his mirror image. I brought the house down . . . in a manner of speaking. But it should really have happened, you know – it should have collapsed on the audience. I made them forget, Robert. Forget themselves and their fellow-men. Forget King Lear, too, for that matter. Towards the end, just before I die, when I came on-stage with the murdered Cordelia in my outstretched arms, to give her into their hands as a final act, as an acknowledgement of people's wickedness, as a reminder of what we call a conscience, they were too busy applauding to receive her.

Good God, Edmund, you don't know what you're saying . . .

Oh yes, he said, I know very well what I'm saying, and I also know that even this time, when I gave more than I've ever been able to, I failed to reach the human being within them. . . . Do you hear them knocking on the door there? You know as well as I do what they want. If I let them in, they'll shower me with their intoxicating enthusiasm for my superb movement on the stage and my beautiful, kingly voice. Some will also ask if they can touch me, and – entranced – they'll run their fingers over the soft ermine round my hood. . . . But the scream, Robert, the scream from King Lear's shredded soul – no one will mention that. Because they didn't hear it! Even you didn't hear it. Even you especially, my dear Robert.

That was when you shot him, said the guest almost inaudibly.

Robert Turner didn't answer immediately, but with his hand made a little sign to the head waiter, who stood ready under a plane tree a short distance from the table. The head waiter nodded to a young waiter at the entrance to the restaurant, and as the waiter came promptly towards them between the tables, carrying the dish with the stuffed capon, Robert Turner said: It makes no difference who did the shooting. Actually, he was dead as a human being long before he left the stage – something I should have seen, you know, even before the first curtain.

Then they ate the castrated cock.

THE FIFTH
EVENING

回 回 回 回 回

WHEN the emaciated man, who now felt himself more and more to be Joseph Frost, returned to the hotel after he had eaten the stuffed capon as Robert Turner's guest, he discovered that once more there was a letter for him in his pigeon-hole at the reception desk. But this time he didn't even ask for the letter, and when the receptionist wanted to give it to him, he said it could just stay there. Neither before he fell asleep that night nor after he had awakened the next morning did he think very much about what could be in it, but rather about the fact that it didn't concern him, because he was no longer the man he had been before he began to feel he was Joseph Frost.

Nevertheless, the letter was by no means without significance, because it made him feel he had to go the whole way and sever himself completely from the person he had once been. In short, he had to burn every bridge – something he thought he had heard that artists did not infrequently in order to find their true self. In films he had seen how Paul Gauguin had suddenly gone to some South Sea island or other, and in a newspaper he had once read about an American who one day had taken his hat and coat and left home without a word, and not a soul had heard anything from him until he had become a famous writer many years later.

Since he was already staying on a foreign island, where no one – not even Robert Turner – knew him as the man he once had been, no journey was necessary. All he needed to do

was to move to another place in that little town and not leave
a new address, so that no letters could be forwarded to him. For
that reason he walked about in the streets all morning looking
for a new place to stay, and at last he found a room in the home
of a family who usually rented to people who couldn't afford a
hotel.

That the room was small and furnished only with a
wardrobe, an old iron bed, a table and a chair didn't bother him
at all, but merely tied up with the feeling he had of being Joseph
Frost. Moved, he saw himself sitting at the table writing, while
now and then he cast a glance towards the courtyard outside
his window, where an orange tree and a plane tree fought for
the sunlight that shone in between the gables of houses. During
the afternoon he packed, settled up at the hotel and went to
his new room without bringing the letter, which still lay in
the pigeon-hole at the reception desk. The receptionist tried
to run after him with it, but too late. He had already swung
into another street, so the receptionist just stood there on the
steps with the letter in his hand.

For some reason or other, perhaps because he had more
difficulty in feeling like Joseph Frost when he sat opposite
Robert Turner, he didn't mention anything to his host at
dinner that evening about his having moved. The change of
which moving was a concrete expression – as dramatic as
taking one's hat and coat and leaving home without a word
– made him think about what he suspected had happened to
Robert Turner before he came to the Aegean islands. Hadn't
he said that he had been dead and then brought to life again?
And wasn't a rebirth exactly what he himself felt would be
happening to him in the little room to which he had moved?

He had been so absorbed in thinking about what had
really happened to Robert Turner that he hadn't paid any
attention to what food his host had ordered. He gathered,
however, that the first course must be some kind of salad,
for Robert Turner expressed himself rather sarcastically about
the restaurant's kitchen, which hadn't even the most ordinary
vegetables on hand, and about the head waiter's need to seek
assistance again at his cousin's – this time to obtain decent

yoghurt for a *tzatziki*, the only dish with which Robert Turner would consider beginning the meal that evening. Out of consideration for his guest, he said, he had ordered as a main course an *ochtapodi krassato*, without eating which one couldn't visit these islands, and strangely enough they had had the octopus, of which this ragout is made, soaking in water overnight, so that the cousin was spared supplying that too.

And to please you still more, Robert Turner added, I thought we could finish for once with a cup of coffee prepared the way they have been doing it here on these coasts for several hundred years – so thick, you almost have to eat it with a spoon. If you fancy, you can have *karidhopitta* as well, a splendid cake with walnuts and raisins, but myself, I think such sweet things lie too heavy in the stomach at the end of a meal.

The guest looked at Robert Turner and knew that he should have thanked his host for this thoughtfulness, which perhaps was intended to make up for the painful incident of the evening before, when he had almost been compelled to order blindly a soup he had never eaten. But it was impossible for him to think about anything but Robert Turner's incomprehensible death and resurrection, and because they had to wait for the soup anyhow, he plucked up courage at last and managed to ask how it had really happened.

Perhaps it sounds strange, Robert Turner said and took a drink of the local wine that the head waiter had begun placing on the table without even waiting for the order, but to speak frankly I look on my death as a fairly trivial episode. On the other hand, I probably shouldn't conceal the fact that it was an interesting experience, with aspects, moreover, that were to a certain extent surprising. I have in mind what you might call my resurrection.

The background was that fire I was telling you about some evenings ago, in so far as people thought I had set fire to the manor in order to kill my wife, Lady Euphemia. It is in itself an indisputable fact that she died in the fire, and I shan't say that it made any difference to me worth mentioning, but if

I had wanted to kill her, I would undoubtedly have chosen a considerably less dramatic method. The idea that I would have destroyed for ever such a beautiful building and an irreplaceable art collection merely to transport a single person to eternity is naturally a laughable absurdity which merely reveals ordinary people's lack of values and sense of proportion.

I shan't tire you with a description of the tedious trial, merely mention a few details that may be of interest. It's obvious that death, especially when it's a result of murder, makes a strangely disturbing impression on most people. Even my defence counsel, Sir Charles Bradbury, whom I had known for years as a level-headed man, would have liked me to show despair all the time over Lady Euphemia's death. Of course I realize that his being able to allude to such despair would have been an advantage during the trial, but it amazed me that he seemed to expect such an emotion from me even when we were alone. There were even moments when he clearly thought I should express remorse – something I found highly bewildering. Quite by chance, you see, I had been of assistance to him some years earlier in finding an artist to paint a portrait of his wife. The confidential talks we had in this connection about his relationship with her – which at that point of time was a trifle disturbed by an affair he was having with a very young, but rather ungifted ballerina at the opera – told me that the thought of her early death was by no means alien to him. To tell you the truth, I envisaged the portrait as a sort of preparation, so that afterwards one wouldn't quite forget what she had looked like. It struck me during the trial that it was probably his own conscience more than mine which lay behind his need for my contrition, and I find it not unreasonable that a similar state of affairs held good, too, for the other people taking part in the proceedings.

Another point that will perhaps interest you is whether the child was named during the trial, since there wouldn't have been a fire without her help. But naturally not a word was said about my Eurydice's participation. Even Sir Charles never came to know about her, not just to spare the child, whose whereabouts I didn't know anyway, but perhaps first and foremost because he would hardly have believed me. Besides, with his predilection for young dancers, he would probably have misconstrued the relationship and interpreted it as an additional reason for my having wanted Lady Euphemia out of the way. Considering the child's age, it is even conceivable he would have thought that I abused minors and that he would have withdrawn from the case in middle-class revulsion. Both judge and jury would probably have had a similar attitude.

Nothing of this, however, would have affected me, for the outcome of the case was in fact quite unimportant to me. The feeling of relief – of having been freed from my earthly goods – that overwhelmed me when I stood in the grounds and looked at the sea of flame wore off surprisingly fast, you see, and was replaced by a feeling of nothingness that is almost indescribable. It was as if, without the child's presence, I simply had no inner existence, and the loss of those beautiful rooms and those marvellous paintings filled me with a sorrow I had never felt before. Life as such became, if I may say so, more meaningless than ever, because all the results of my work had been destroyed. You will surely object that, of course, I must still have had my knowledge and my love of art, but it was as if both the knowledge and the love of art were no more, because their visible expressions no longer existed. As I sat in that grey cell, or when I found myself in the dock in the court-room, I was a person robbed of all that had given meaning to my life. I felt the way an artist must if every single one of his works has been destroyed, and to the extent that I was capable of thinking, I thought I understood why Rouault and Gauguin burned their paintings when death approached. Nothingness must be complete, if one is to get peace in one's grave.

One might have thought, perhaps, that I would have been bitter towards my mind's liberating Joan of Arc – and there were times certainly when I asked myself why she had come into my life – but for the most part I felt no bitterness at all. For even in my deepest experience of non-existence – more bare than any cell can be – I still distantly remembered to begin with her hand against my cheek in the churchyard, my presumptuous happiness during my walk with her to the estate and the intense feeling of liberation, of being my real and innermost self, when the fire consumed the outer me that I had created for myself. But, as I said, the memory was distant, and it became more and more distant with each day that passed behind the prison wall. At last it disappeared – the way a candle burns out and dies with a little flicker and leaves behind an utter, ice-cold darkness. Sometimes I tried to call her back before my inner eye, but I couldn't even remember how she looked or, after a while, even that she had existed.

My own sense of not existing marked my behaviour in a way that must have influenced the jury's verdict more than anything else. I met with amused indifference my energetic counsel's desperate attempt to coax despair out of me. Then after the counsel for the prosecution had pointed out the cynical element in my painstakingly prepared murder of a woman he said I had entirely to thank for the position I had attained, I expressed my hearty agreement with him, and when he asked in alarm if I had no human feelings, I replied that feeling was a notion I knew only from literature's most naïve productions.

To say that I wanted to be executed is perhaps an exaggeration, but when sentence was pronounced and I was condemned to death by hanging, I took it with an almost cheerful composure, which both court and press looked on as confirmation of the view people had formed of my soul as absolutely ice-cold and callous. In the days between the passing of the sentence and my execution, they watched me keenly for at least some small sign of despair and fear of death, as if the punishment would be pointless if I didn't show such feelings – and it's not to be denied that the newspaper headlines characterized me in a not very flattering manner, which in other circumstances I should probably have taken much to heart. My relationship with Sir Charles also became rather cool when it dawned on him that neither would I appeal against the sentence nor did I want to seek a pardon – but it's reasonable, for that matter, that he regarded my indifference and my lack of will to co-operate as the principal reason why his efforts as defence counsel proved so befuddled that on several occasions there were hints of laughter in the court-room.

My execution itself was such an embarrassing affair that I see no reason to devote many words to it. A hangman in our day naturally doesn't have very much experience, but I had nevertheless expected a more professional performance, and I must confess that I felt as if I were participating in the rehearsal of a crime film of fairly dubious quality. It even got to the stage that I had to lend a hand in making the noose slide properly – surely a victim should be spared having to pitch in like that, even if, naturally, it's always a pleasure to be of service.

If you ask at this point what I felt at the moment of death or how existence after death turned out, I shall probably disappoint you by saying that none of it was especially remarkable either, but almost as uninteresting as I had imagined it beforehand. The pain when the rope tightened and my neck had obviously snapped lasted such a short time that I can hardly remember it, and after that the customary laws of nature were simply repealed. I was there, but nevertheless not there in the sense that I could see myself, for example, from a particular part of the room, and the notion of time existed no more. That time didn't exist I thought was actually rather gratifying, for then the tedium of merely being passively present had no duration and therefore became less tiring. How it would have turned out if I had been buried I naturally don't know, but it's possible, of course, that the missing distinction between eternity and the instant would have been a strain.

Do you know how long you were in the morgue? his guest asked, with a feeling of strange bewilderment at how natural it was to ask a question which in reality was entirely opposed to the laws of nature.

While I lay there, I had no perception of that – as of course you should have understood – but afterwards I realized that about a day passed before the child found me and brought me back to life again. Just as after a dream, the details of this incident are unclear to me. I merely realized that something was happening and had a vague feeling of the child's presence, but it was only when I opened my eyes that I found my Eurydice in the physical sense. . . . Though I suppose I should call her my Orphea, as if she were a female Orpheus, for the roles were exchanged, you know. It's possible that her presence alone had been enough to bring me back to life, but I imagine she took my head in her hands and let them slide down my neck, so that the youthful strength and steadfast warmth within her healed it and made my heart beat again. Later, out of pure curiosity, I had X-ray pictures taken of my neck, and there's not a trace of a break.

As you would expect, I was both stiff and frozen after having lain naked in the refrigerated drawer, and it was therefore a stroke of good luck that my Orphea had been thoughtful enough to bring along my clothes, which she had found in the prison. How I would have felt about such a resurrection if my Orphea hadn't been there isn't easy to say, but in all likelihood I should have been highly irritated at returning to a state of nothingness. With the child at my side, however, I felt the same liberating lightness, the same intense experience of existence through merely being myself, as when we had stood looking at the fire, and in spite of my age I felt like a youngster overwhelmed by being alive when she let us out of the morgue and we ran off down the street at dawn before they found out what had happened.

What did they do when they did find out?

Robert Turner smiled to himself while he poured wine into his glass and then drank from it slowly, as if the enjoyment of the wine was an expression of the sorrowless existence the resurrection had brought.

I haven't the foggiest notion, he said, but I assume they were rather surprised. Rather like those Roman soldiers who found the tomb empty. Naturally without comparison in other respects. The interesting thing was that the papers didn't print a single word about my corpse disappearing. They probably felt it was so inexplicable that they chose to keep it a deep secret. Anyway, it can't be denied either that it would have looked bad for our well-esteemed prison service if it came to light that hanged criminals can just climb from the refrigerated drawers and wander out of doors.

The only thing about this that troubled me, Robert Turner went on, was that the child – my rescuing Orphea

– disappeared. My intention was that after I had carried out certain small economic transactions, we would leave the country as quickly as possible, but amidst the hectic activity she simply vanished. Naturally it's conceivable that she didn't want to go with me, that she felt her work was accomplished after she had given me back my life. But for me it was a tragedy, though oddly enough not so great a one as you might imagine, for since the incident in the morgue I've felt that she will always hold her hand over me, even if, physically, she's not here, and in my mind she's with me all the time as a spiritual companion.

Even so, you're looking for her, said his guest.

Robert Turner looked down, and for the first time in the days they had known each other, the guest saw that his host showed signs of despair. He raised his glass, but put it down again without drinking, and after he had sat looking at it for a while, he said: That, my dear Frost, is because it gets more and more difficult to recall her. I know that she's still inside me, and on our first evening I managed to describe her from memory, but I can't see her clearly any more – the way I can see you – and I could do so for several years after that night in the morgue. Sometimes it feels like an unbearable loss, a pain I would compare to what an artist feels when his talent threatens to desert him. When he can no longer glimpse his muse. I'm about to return to nothingness, and lately my dread of this has driven me from one place to another in the hope of finding her.

Then he raised his head and looked at his guest. You will undoubtedly object, he said, that she may have changed – that in the course of these years she will have become a young woman who has long since lost her unwavering concern for me and may even have forgotten the churchyard, the fire and the morgue. Even so, I have a need to meet her again, for maybe in her eyes I'll see once more my innermost, living self.

Again the food was brought, as if at a secret sign from Robert Turner, or perhaps the head waiter, in the course of these evenings, had learned to recognize when Robert Turner or his guest approached the end of a story, and again they ate in silence. Of course the guest was used to eating without talking, for at home they no longer had anything to say to one another, either at table or in other situations, but he had always dreamed about happy meals with laughter and cheerful conversation. When he cast cautious glances towards the other tables on the pavement outside the restaurant, he saw that some of the guests at any rate smiled and laughed and talked together while they ate and sipped their wine. He noticed in particular a young couple who sat under a carob tree a short distance away. A meal, he thought, is a uniting action, and their pleasure from the food enhances in a way the experience they have of each other. Naturally he couldn't hear what they said, but he saw their smiles and the faint flush in their cheeks when they whispered confidences to each other. It was the woman he noticed especially. She was scarcely twenty years old, and her features were too coarse for her to be called pretty. But her eyes – in fact, every movement – radiated a warmth and a strength that made one appreciate that beauty is something other than, and perhaps more than, flawlessness and perfect features. Sometimes she looked over at him and Robert Turner, and once she even met his eye. Afterwards she bent towards her friend and said something. Maybe she's saying, thought the guest, that sitting over there are two old men who have known each other for so many years that they no longer have anything to talk about. But if so, she was wrong, for of course it wasn't a question of years, but of barely five days, and seldom had the guest talked so much as in the course of these evenings. He looked up at Robert Turner, and again he felt a kind of aversion. The manner in which his host cut up his food and studied the pieces before he put them in his mouth to savour them while he chewed slowly and painstakingly was an enjoyment of his own bodily senses that shut out everything else, not only conversation with the person with whom he was dining.

Procuring yoghurt from the head waiter's cousin had taken so long that the octopus ragout was placed on the table at the same moment as they finished the salad, and Robert Turner said that the new story – which he had been looking forward to hearing his guest tell all day – would unfortunately have to be postponed until before they had their coffee. In contrast to his conduct during the previous day's meal, the guest ate both the first and the main courses this evening, despite the fact that the octopus in particular tasted too unfamiliar for him to like it, and as usual he had finished long before Robert Turner. It was as if the move to the little room had given him a kind of peace and an almost fatalistic belief that he would manage to tell a new story, as was expected of him. The expectation, therefore, didn't feel so frightening a demand as it had before, but like a stimulus to the coming of the words. He hadn't even thought about what story he would try to tell. Though there before the window facing the courtyard with the orange tree and the plane tree he had suddenly seen before him something that he had once experienced and that in one period of his life had filled him with the strangest dreams and thoughts. Yes, curiously enough, he actually remembered the dreams and the thoughts better than the experience itself. So when Robert Turner had finished eating and had told the head waiter that they would like a cup of Greek coffee when they had digested their food, it was the guest's turn for once to lean back and let a story take form.

Mogens Klint, began the guest, hadn't been to the zoo since he was a child. He happened to have been brought there then because Sunday morning could hang heavy in a cramped flat in the middle of Copenhagen and because his parents seemed to have heard that children should experience animals.

Excuse me for interrupting, said Robert Turner, but it strikes me that you always write about the same person. Can't you be inventive when it comes to characters, or is there some significance in this tiresome repetition? In that case, you ought surely to have made him somewhat more inspiring poetically – someone who could have given the imagination a bit of a lift-off. Every time you describe him I see before me grey backyards, half-dirty children, pale men with bowed heads queuing up outside job centres, women without charm. In short, that kind of so-called social realism some artists in the first half of this century tried to produce to show that they were of use in society by displaying sympathy for a lower class they neither belonged to nor in their heart felt appreciably attracted by.

The emaciated man looked straight in front of him and said: Maybe that's the grey kind of man he is.

Well of course that's your affair, said Robert Turner. I merely felt it was my duty to call your attention to an artistic weakness. But to return to your story – this Mogens Klint, as far as I understand, had been to a zoo as a child to experience animals.

Yes, but in actual fact it wasn't animals he experienced, for Sunday was the very day there were usually so many people at the zoo that he hardly caught sight of the animals, and if he did manage to see any, they were, naturally enough, behind bars or in deep pits. So he grew tired, began to cry and had to be soothed with buns or some other treat that his parents really hadn't the means to buy. For that reason they visited the zoo more and more rarely, and at last he had almost forgotten it existed.

But then one day, many years later, he went to the zoo by sheer chance. It wasn't to look at the animals at all, but to find a place where he could sit alone and think. Because it was an ordinary afternoon in autumn, there was hardly a person there, but it was cold, so he walked through the door of a building to get a bit of warmth into his body. He had entered the Big Cats' House, a large room with a bench running the length of the one long wall and with cages along the other. Numb with cold, he sank down on the bench.

Where he sat thinking, I assume? said Robert Turner.

That's right.

About what?

It could have been about a lot of things.

Robert Turner raised his eyebrows. We've been through this before, he said with conspicuous mildness, namely, that a work of art must not raise questions that aren't answered. That leads to uneasiness and confusion, not recognition and harmony, which it is the artist's foremost duty to create. Therefore, one must know what this Mogens Klint sat thinking about. Was it perhaps about suicide, which is always interesting? Or was it about how he would kill his wife?

It wasn't about suicide at any rate, the story-teller said in a low voice. After sitting there for a while, perhaps without getting his thoughts collected at all, Mogens Klint discovered something he couldn't exactly understand. He didn't believe his own eyes, as they say. In the cage directly opposite him there was a beautiful leopard, and it suddenly dawned on him that there was a little dog lying asleep on a kind of hay-bed where the leopard probably should have been lying. The leopard, which was not only five times bigger than the dog but also young and powerful, could easily have killed that little dog with a single blow of its paw. But it didn't. Instead, it sat in a corner of the cage and trembled.

The truth was, but Mogens Klint had no suspicion of it, that the little dog belonged to one of the keepers in the Big Cats' House, and that from time to time it was used to suckle young lions, tigers and leopards that couldn't be kept alive by other means. She was especially well suited to this, not only because she was continually whelping and had a lot of milk, but above all because she had such shaggy fur that the big cats' claws didn't harm her, and she was so prized as a foster-mother that, when new-born, the beautiful leopard had been sent all the way from Rome to Copenhagen to be suckled by her.

By the afternoon Mogens Klint discovered the little dog, the leopard's suckling had long since ceased, but in the belief that it amused the public, the keepers often let the two animals remain together all the same. However, the little dog was accustomed, like most dogs, to push her troublesome puppies aside the moment they had been weaned, while the leopard tried to get its foster-mother to join it in the playful, considerate training in the hunt that young leopards receive from their mothers. With increasing desperation, Mogens Klint saw how the leopard again and again walked over to the half-sleeping dog and nudged her affectionately with its muzzle, only to be met by bared teeth and and angry growling. Each time, the leopard drew back terrified. It squeezed itself up in a corner of the cage and sat there trembling so that all its slender body shook.

For more than four hours, right up to the zoo's closing-time, Mogens Klint sat and looked at this strange drama, and on the way home he felt a mounting hatred of the little dog – this loathsome creature that was so shaggy you couldn't tell her front from her behind except when she showed her teeth and growled. A creeping thing that buried herself in the hay and pressed her eyes tight shut instead of coming out to the beautiful young leopard who ceaselessly, and each time with the same touching expectancy, sought a mother's care.

That night Mogens Klint began to dream about the leopard. Although what was dream and what was longing and imagination is not easy to say, for at the same time as he played with the leopard in the shadow of the acacias, he could see his wife rolled up in a sort of foetal position at his side and hear her snorting breath. They raced each other over the savannas, the leopard and he – rolled with each other in the tall grass, while the beautiful big cat stroked him gently with supple paws or took his arm, foot or neck in its mouth without its awl-sharp teeth leaving behind so much as a scratch. At last he laughed, drew the young animal close to him and laid his face against the lovely, soft fur.

In the morning he was restless and said, if possible, still less than usual to his wife and two teenage children, and at his desk in the little shipping firm in a back street in Amager, where he had worked longer than he could remember, he couldn't concentrate on the columns of figures in front of him. They somehow dissolved and let the leopard, the savanna and the acacias emerge like a mirage, and when his hands approached the sheets of paper or the arm-rests of his badly worn chair, it was as if his skin were kindled by the leopard's supple touch.

So when the working day was over he didn't go home, but went directly to the Big Cats' House in the zoo. Despite the fact that he knew the young leopard wouldn't recognize him, he thought the amber-yellow eyes turned towards him beseechingly when he sat down on the bench directly opposite the cage. Was it possible that the animal sensed his sympathetic desperation? Or that in the night, contrary to all physical laws, it had broken away from its cage and bounded over the savanna with him – had lain at his side in the tall grass and rested its coal-black muzzle against his neck?

The little dog lay rolled up in the hay that afternoon too, and when the leopard seemed for a moment to be approaching a piece of meat that lay on the floor of the cage, the repulsive creature growled warningly, rose slowly, walked over to the piece of meat and began to eat, while the leopard sat trembling in the corner where it usually sat. The little dog relaxed. With great care, as if she were choosing the best each time, she tore small pieces from the meat and chewed for a long time before swallowing. When at last there was no more left, she sank down on something that was supposed to be her tail and sat there looking vacantly at the people beyond the bars, while at regular intervals she licked her lips.

Even as Mogens Klint felt the fury rise in him at the sight of that loathsomely bristling creature, it astonished him that no one else saw what was going on. It seemed they simply didn't notice the little dog. Finally he could bear it no longer and tried to draw people's attention to the fact that there was a little dog sitting in there with the leopard. But they appeared not to understand what he was saying, for they merely glanced at him and hurried on.

Directly beyond Mogens Klint, an artist stood sketching the head of a tiger that lay in the cage beside the leopard's. This artist, as a matter of fact, had tried for many years to do a picture of a tiger, but although for an entire winter he had accompanied a travelling German circus which had a tiger as a special attraction, he hadn't managed to get to the tiger's head in the picture. So exhaustively had he studied the big predator that he had even been shut in the cage with it by accident, but that hadn't brought him closer to completing his painting. Afterwards he had received a grant from the Danish government to finish it once and for all, and so he had settled down in Copenhagen because he had found in the zoo there a tiger that was as big and terrifying as the one he had been shut in with.

Mogens Klint bent a bit forward towards the artist. What breed do you think that dog is? he asked, as if making conversation, for he didn't want to give the impression that he thought someone whose craft was observation hadn't noticed her like the rest.

What dog?

The little dog in there with the leopard.

Cut the crap, said the artist without lifting his eyes from his sketch-book. How can there be a little dog in with the leopard?

Now listen, said Mogens Klint. I'm telling you there *is* a little dog in that cage. She's just eaten all the leopard's food, and now she's sitting right in front of you licking her lips. I asked you what breed she can be.

The artist threw a glance at him. Fine, that's fine, he said a bit soothingly and began to pack up his sketching gear. So there's a little dog in with the leopard?

Just look for yourself! shouted Mogens Klint.

The shaggy creature clearly didn't like anyone to shout, for she emitted a sharp little yelp. The artist, who was then making a quick exit with his sketch-book under his arm, turned round sharply and stared at the animal. By God, he burst out, there *is* a little dog in there!

The story-teller stopped, not to let the artist's outburst linger a moment for effect, but because each muscle in his body was tense with a kind of dread of how his story would end and because his mouth was dry. His hand a little unsteady, he filled his glass with the local Greek wine and drained it.

Well, your story has a kind of point at any rate, said Robert Turner when the man had put the glass down again. With the help of the painter you did spotlight the necessity for the artist to concentrate. Naturally he couldn't see this dog when his whole attention had to be directed towards the tiger's beautiful head. . . . That majestic perfection he had sacrificed so much to immortalize. But I think you weaken the whole thing by bringing in the nocturnal manias of this everlasting Mogens Klint – as if anyone would dream about letting himself be embraced by leopards.

The emaciated guest looked down. I haven't finished the story yet, he said.

Good God Almighty, Robert Turner blurted out, must we have still more zoological fantasies? Still, as I have myself asked you to give me some examples of your writing, I suppose I'm obliged to put up with the rest of this. But spare me sodomy, if you don't mind. To write about such relationships between men and beasts is to venture among the dubious attempts of the so-called radicals to establish an identity that's wrenched free from the middle class – which I find extremely primitive.

The next night became even more disturbed, the story-teller continued, reddening slightly but without pursuing Robert Turner's remark about people's relationships with animals. To be sure, neither his wife nor his teenage children noticed Mogens Klint's restless remoteness, but then, broadly speaking, they never noticed him at all anyway. The only thing that struck them was that he didn't come home till after dark and that he therefore couldn't have been home for dinner. Afterwards his wife also seemed to remember that he hadn't tried to look at her when she undressed in the bedroom, but at the time it had merely crossed her mind as a relief, and she hadn't attached any importance to it . . .

Wife! interrupted Robert Turner, suddenly annoyed. You talk all the time about his wife. Doesn't the woman have a name? It's impossible to enter into the spirit of a literary work, especially of something as pointless as this, if the characters don't even have names, which can give the reader a feeling of real life.

Then the emaciated one, who of course called himself Joseph Frost, said: Maybe he had forgotten it.

Robert Turner looked at him quickly. There was something in his guest's voice he hadn't heard before. A defiance, almost a bitterness. Then he shrugged his shoulders somewhat resignedly, as if to give the impression he preferred to ignore the story-teller's romantic attempt to excuse his lack of imagination and hadn't noticed the emotional undertone.

A short while after the bed-light had been put out, continued the emaciated man, Mogens Klint was again out on the savanna, which loomed up in the cramped room and grew through the walls out over the grey, dirty city. Slowly, as if a cloud was gliding away from the moon or his eyes had to grow used to the darkness. There the leopard awaited him. But this night they didn't play with abandoned light-heartedness among the acacias, for now was the time for hunting.

The whole evening Mogens Klint had, in a state of excitement, seen in front of him that loathsome dog which sat licking her lips, and he had thought that in one way or another he must teach the young leopard to capture its own prey – to cease depending on pieces of meat that were flung to it and that the shaggy creature usually just took from it. In the moonlight out on the savanna he therefore placed a hand on the shoulder of the tense animal, while their glance met in expectant excitement, and guided it against the wind up close to a small herd of antelopes. He felt as if he were about to burst with happiness when he saw how the leopard understood his slightest sign and gradually began to steal flat along the ground with the lithe movements and perfect self-control of a wild beast. When they had drawn close enough and he thought that the moment had come, he pressed the excited leopard lightly between the shoulder-blades, and side by side they sprang forward and separated a weak hind from the herd of terrified animals.

She was easy game. With a single blow he snapped the neck of the hind, which lay rolled up on the ground as she gave a few last, snorting breaths. Then he bent down and tore his prey's throat open with his teeth to show the leopard how, and together they lapped up the hot blood that streamed from the wound. After they had taken the entrails out and buried them because of vultures, hyenas and jackals, he taught the leopard how, with head raised, to carry the carcass off to a tree, spring up into it and hang the carcass on a branch high above the ground. Then, when they had eaten what they were able to of the juicy flesh, they fell asleep up there on the branch, close against each other, just before day began to dawn.

Even before Mogens Klint set off for the zoo next afternoon, he fully realized what he had to do. It had come to him as he was sitting at his desk pretending to arrange his papers with the long columns of figures, while all the while he fancied he heard the leopard's wailing from the cage and saw before him at the same time the lithe young beast taking gliding bounds across the savanna. Then almost imperceptibly the landscape began to change in his mind. The acacias turned into beech trees, the dry grass into lush meadows and the antelopes into royal stags and fallow deer that grazed among the ingeniously clipped shrubs of the Hermitage – the royal hunting lodge north of the city.

When he came to the Big Cats' House he didn't walk as usual into the large room with cages along the one wall and a bench along all of the other, but quietly opened a small door marked No Admittance. Inside, as he had imagined, there was a long corridor with steel shutters leading into the different cages. These shutters weren't hinged, as doors usually are, but moved in vertical grooves and could be raised and lowered with the help of a pull-wire attached to a lever on the wall. He knew exactly behind which shutter he would find the leopard, and it was really as much as he could do not to run down to it. But he knew he must be careful, so that a keeper wouldn't discover him, and for that reason he walked slowly along the corridor, listening attentively the whole time. When he finally stopped at the shutter leading in to the leopard, he closed his eyes as if to control the feeling of happiness which was on the point of overwhelming him. He smiled to himself and thought he felt the skin on his face growing smooth and young and the stiffness of age being stroked from his body. Then he gripped the lever with both hands and pulled.

Even before the shutter had come half-way up, the leopard was out in the corridor. Then, with its body pressed against the floor, it bounded off to a large shutter that blocked the cages' exit into the open air surrounding the Big Cats' House. When it realized it could go no further, it turned round sharply and stood there taut as a bowstring and with its ears laid flat, while its tail swung from side to side. It happened so fast that Mogens Klint didn't really grasp what had occurred, and at the same time he saw himself with remarkable clarity, as if from outside – a thin, middle-aged man in a grey overcoat and hat, still smiling and yet with eyes opened wide, who, in his bewilderment, stretched his arms out as if towards a little child.

Then he took a few steps forward, clumsily, as if he wasn't conscious that he was doing it. The leopard bared its teeth and snarled softly before it sprang, and everything went dark for Mogens Klint.

Robert Turner sat so motionless that his guest began to think that he had fallen asleep or that something had happened to him. But then he stretched his right hand towards the table with extreme slowness, took his glass and drank carefully. After putting it down again with equal slowness, he raised his head and looked at his guest.

Unfortunately I've never had a dog, he said, even if Lady Euphemia thought it would have been proper to keep a pair of greyhounds that could have accompanied her around the estate. But of course dogs have been a cherished motif for most of our great painters, so one can say that I know their nature rather well all the same, especially as I have no sentimental memory of any so-called four-legged friend of my own. So in spite of the eternal Mogens Klint, whom you always mix into the things you write, I was actually moved for a moment or two by your story. The description of the dog definitely gave me – if I may put it this way – an impression of some sort of dignity, even if the development was rather flimsy. But the leopard, my dear Frost, the leopard worried me. If you really want to keep it, I would advise you to delay publication, for leopards are not a very popular subject at the moment – especially in highly educated circles. So you will hardly get much joy from bringing the story out now.

Again the guest noticed that the young couple at the table under the carob tree were casting stealthy glances towards them, and he saw the girl bend forward to her friend and, smiling, whisper something to him.

It seems as if those two young people know you, said the guest, and he nodded discreetly in the direction of the carob tree. Maybe they're art students who have attended one of your many lectures and who are down here now to make use of what you've taught them.

But Robert Turner didn't move. He sat on as if wrapped up in his own thoughts without having heard what his guest had said to him. Suddenly he folded his napkin and placed it on the table; then he took some banknotes from his pocket and put them half under his plate.

Unfortunately I can't remember if I mentioned it to you when you came here this evening, he said, but this is our last meal together. I'm leaving this very evening, and now it occurs to me that I must have forgotten to pack some important books – especially a monograph on Praxiteles that I can hardly be without. Reluctant though I am, I must therefore leave you immediately.

As Robert Turner rose, his guest exclaimed: But the coffee you ordered?

You must enjoy that alone, said Robert Turner. In such rewarding company as yours, the time passes incredibly fast, and your story about the dog caused me to forget my departure altogether. I hope those books of yours will be translated one day into a language I've mastered, so I can see if it's just as enriching to read you as it has been to hear you tell stories.

Has the search here been in vain?

Robert Turner looked at him.

The search? Oh yes, naturally, the search for my Eurydice. That's right. It's been completely in vain. She's probably staying on Melos instead – something I should have thought of long ago. I remember her being especially moved by what I told her about the beautiful art treasures they've found there – not least the famous Venus.

After a little pause, he took his guest's hand. To be frank with you, it pains me for us to part so quickly, he said, for it has been a pleasure to make your acquaintance. . . . No, no, not at all! *I* am the one who must say thanks. My conversations with you under this beautiful evening sky have restored my faith in *homo sincerus* – the frank, sincere human being. Then he added smiling: But remember what I said about the leopard! Another year, perhaps, leopards will be the very thing to write about to gain recognition in educated circles.

After his host had gone, the guest – who was no longer a guest – sat and waited for the coffee. He thought about how he would have spent these evenings if he hadn't met this generous man, if he had gained no insight into a world he had never seen before and, for that matter, would never get to see again. At the same time he was ashamed of himself, for hadn't Robert Turner's last words been that these conversations had restored his faith in the frank, sincere human being! Why was it that he hadn't been able to tell the truth, that he was neither a writer nor a man named Joseph Frost, despite his feeling of shame? How could he, without restraint, have deceived such a trusting person in that way? And how could he also – almost, at any rate – have deceived himself? For little by little he had of course felt like this Joseph Frost and had even believed he was a kind of writer or at least could become one.

This gnawing feeling of shame oppressed the emaciated man so powerfully that he was unaware of the girl from the table under the carob tree until she stood directly beside him and said: May I ask you something?

Of course, he said and reddened because he had been too preoccupied and confused to get up for her, but managed nevertheless to add: Won't you sit down?

Without taking her eyes from him – as if she were afraid that he, too, would somehow disappear – she sat down cautiously on the chair where Robert Turner had just been sitting and asked: That man who's left, was he a friend of yours?

He who had called himself Joseph Frost didn't quite know what he should answer – for what *is* a friend? Actually he had never had any, and at least he hadn't in his entire life talked so long with one and the same person as he had done at these dinners. On the other hand you don't lie to a friend, do you, as he had done?

It's difficult for me to say if we were friends, he replied, but perhaps he considered me one, for he was so utterly frank with me and spoke so openly about himself. But actually I met Professor Turner only a few days ago, and after that I've merely been his guest and dined with him here for several hours each evening.

The girl stared at him, then burst into laughter. Fantastic! she said. Did he really call himself Turner?

Why shouldn't he?

The young girl looked down for a moment, as if to collect herself, and without understanding why, he thought there was something familiar about her. If she hadn't been sitting in front of him in a white, short-sleeved blouse and a pair of worn jeans, he thought, she could have been a sculpture he had seen once, a sculpture shaped by strong, quick hands. But she was very far from being a sculpture, and when she looked up again – quite serious this time – he was struck by a warmth he had seldom seen in a young person. In a flash he seemed to remember from where he knew her, but then it went out of his head.

You can't have been in England early one summer six years ago, she said, because then you would have understood why I thought it was so fantastic he actually called himself Turner. The papers were filled with pictures of him at the time and with reports of what he had done. He's a bit plumper now and has got a grey beard, but I recognized him almost the moment I sat down at the table over there.

That was at the time the professor was hanged, I suppose?

Hanged? said the young girl. No one's been hanged in England during my lifetime – not he or anyone else. And you called him a professor, but he was no more a professor than I was. He was simply a guard at the Tate Gallery – which, among other things, is famous for its big collection of Turner paintings. That was why I had to laugh, because the whole thing began with the stealing of the three most valuable of these paintings and your friend the museum guard disappearing at the same time. Though of course the story was more complicated than that. If you have time, I'll be glad to tell it to you.

The man who for five evenings now had been Robert Turner's guest – or, to put it more accurately, had let himself be fed and entertained by a former museum guard who wasn't called that at all – just barely managed to nod. He had of course heard what the young girl had said, but he didn't understand it. Simply couldn't grasp that this man, who had spellbound him with his knowledge and his moving stories drawn from his life in a world that his guest had only dared dream about, had been turned into a thief and a liar with a few words from a young girl's mouth. What about their solemn agreement of utter frankness? Which of the two should he believe?

A couple of days before the paintings disappeared, the young girl began, the guard who told you he was called Turner sent word to the gallery that he was ill and would have to stay at home for a week or more. So they didn't give him a thought when they discovered one morning that the three pictures had disappeared. On the whole he was a person you barely noticed. People were hardly aware he came to work – invisible and round-shouldered and seedy as he was – and once in a while when he was away, they only noted it because then they were one guard short. True enough, there was a bit in one of the papers about somebody trying to get a few shillings from museum visitors one afternoon because he had told them about Turner and Constable and some other artists as if he were a guide, and about his staying away then for a while because the other guards had laughed at him so much. But by and large, as I told you, he made no more impression than a chair or a spot on the wall.

The theft was – and remained – an inexplicable mystery, and the only thing they gradually realized was that it must have been committed by someone who knew the gallery inside out – one or more of the guards, for instance. Even so, the shabby guard wasn't in anyone's mind till it eventually struck them that he simply hadn't turned up again after his sick-leave. When the police and all the reporters rushed off to his little two-room flat, he wasn't there, and not only that, all his belongings were gone. Then they finally realized how it all must tie together. A good while beforehand, the guard no one had previously thought about had said he was ill and couldn't come to work, then he had let himself in with keys he had had made for himself on the quiet, turned off the alarm system and wandered out with the paintings as easy as anything.

What happened afterwards no one ever got straight, for in spite of the front-page headlines – which set practically the whole country in action – and even if the police did all they could, both the paintings and the guard remained missing without a trace. Finally they found evidence that he had got out of the country, and they assumed the pictures were sold in either France or America, where after a while they were probably hung on the quiet in the home of some well-off collector. They never saw the guard again – but even if he hardly got the full price for the paintings, he's sure to have made quite enough on them to live a carefree life for the rest of his days in some out-of-the-way part of the world.

But, said the man who would perhaps never again feel he was Joseph Frost, how can you be certain it was really him? Six years ago you were only a child, after all. A story like that can't possibly have interested you much then – and newspaper pictures are of poor quality and easy to forget for that reason. I'm certain you've made a mistake.

The young girl smiled faintly. There's something I haven't told you yet, she said. Just before all this happened, I met him once in a churchyard. I was taking care of my mother's grave and I noticed a shabby man who was trying to put a nearby plot in order. The weeds covered everything, almost even covered a small, half-rotten wooden cross, and he seemed completely helpless as he knelt there trying to weed the plot, so he could plant something that must have been a rose-bush. After a while when I walked past to get water, I offered to help him, and while he rested on a bench a short distance from the grave, I cleared away enough of the weeds at least to let me put the bush into the ground. I don't remember what was on the cross, but he told me that it was his daughter lying there and that he had had no one else in life but her.

Do you mean he wasn't even married? asked her listener, and he remembered with a strange feeling of superiority the letter which, unopened, he had torn to pieces and thrown into the waste-paper basket and the one he had even refused to take from the hotel receptionist. For the first time, with a kind of longing for a fellowship he had perhaps never dared experience, he thought uneasily about what might have been in them.

As far as I understood, said the girl, his wife was dead, too – or maybe she had only left him. In any case I got the impression he was alone, and as he sat there on the bench he began to talk – pretty incoherently and really more to himself than to me – about how he would try to save enough one day to go to the islands in the Aegean Sea. I asked where that was and why he wanted to go there. Then he said something I didn't understand much of – about its being a place where over two thousand years ago they had created an art so beautiful that you forgot everything else in the world. He also talked about the crystal-clear green water and the marvellous light and the evening sky, and he told me a legend about someone who brought his beloved up from the kingdom of death.

His Eurydice, her listener said softly.

The young girl got up slowly. Yes, she said. I've realized since that it must have been the legend of Orpheus and Eurydice, and when I walk past the grave now and then on the way to my mother's, I think that he himself was a kind of Orpheus who tried to call back to life the only one he had ever loved. Then she added: When I saw him sitting here with you just now, it seemed for a moment that he recognized me. After he had glanced towards the table where I was sitting, he stiffened a bit, and when you spoke to him afterwards he didn't hear. But he left without looking at me again.

The emaciated man looked at her and asked: Did you stroke his cheek . . . that time?

She raised her head and stood there looking out towards the ruins of the Crusaders' castle and the fishing-boats that were already heading out into the darkness of the night. Yet it seemed as if what she saw was something other than the idyllic harbour, and he tried to glean from the expression on her face what was happening in her mind. From the eyes that suddenly stared, only to be lowered just as quickly. From the lips that became soft and parted slightly, then closed immediately hard and tight. Was it the memory of what happened in the churchyard that fought for power over her? Fought to be relived? At last there was clearly something that won or maybe lost, for her face slowly composed itself and became the way it had been when he discovered her at his table.

Then she turned towards him. No, she said. Should I have?